Winning the
Single Mom's Heart

WINNING THE SINGLE MOM'S HEART

LINDA GOODNIGHT

THORNDIKE
CHIVERS

This Large Print edition is published by Thorndike Press, Waterville, Maine, USA and by BBC Audiobooks Ltd, Bath, England.

Thorndike Press, a part of Gale, Cengage Learning.

The text of this Large Print edition is unabridged.

Other aspects of the book may vary from the original edition.

Set in 16 pt. Plantin.

Printed on permanent paper.

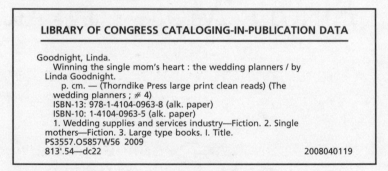

LIBRARY OF CONGRESS CATALOGING-IN-PUBLICATION DATA

Goodnight, Linda.
 Winning the single mom's heart : the wedding planners / by
Linda Goodnight.
  p. cm. — (Thorndike Press large print clean reads) (The
wedding planners ; # 4)
  ISBN-13: 978-1-4104-0963-8 (alk. paper)
  ISBN-10: 1-4104-0963-5 (alk. paper)
  1. Wedding supplies and services industry—Fiction. 2. Single
mothers—Fiction. 3. Large type books. I. Title.
PS3557.O5857W56 2009
813'.54—dc22   2008040119

BRITISH LIBRARY CATALOGUING-IN-PUBLICATION DATA AVAILABLE

Published in 2009 in the U.S. by arrangement with Harlequin Books S.A.
Published in 2009 in the U.K. by arrangement with Harlequin Enterprises II B.V.

U.K. Hardcover: 978 1 408 41247 3 (Chivers Large Print)
U.K. Softcover: 978 1 408 41248 0 (Camden Large Print)

Printed in the United States of America
1 2 3 4 5 6 7 12 11 10 09 08

THE WEDDING PLANNERS

Planning perfect weddings . . . finding happy endings!

In October: *Sweetheart Lost and Found*
by Shirley Jump
Florist: Will Callie catch a bouquet, and reunite with her childhood sweetheart?

In November: *The Heir's Convenient Wife*
by Myrna Mackenzie
Photographer: Regina's wedding album is perfect. Now she needs her husband to say I love you!

In December: *SOS Marry Me!*
by Melissa McClone
Designer: Serena's already made her dress, but a rebel has won her heart. . . .

**In January: *Winning the Single Mom's Heart*
by Linda Goodnight**
Chef: Who will Natalie cut her own wedding cake with?

**In February: *Millionaire Dad, Nanny Needed!*
by Susan Meier**
Accountant: Will Audra's budget for the big day include a millionaire groom?

**In March: *The Bridegroom's Secret*
by Melissa James**
Planner: Julie's always been the wedding planner — will she ever be the bride?

Natalie is the chef who makes cakes for The Wedding Belles. Here are her tips for personal touches that will make your own wedding cake unique and special:

- Unless you are an experienced baker, start with your favorite cake mix instead of baking from scratch. It will taste good, take less time and be more likely to turn out well. You can even make each layer a different flavor! Three layers — a six-inch, an eight-inch and a ten-inch layer — should feed fifty guests.

- Freeze the layers after they have been baked and cooled. This makes frosting and decorating much easier, without the fear of tearing your layers.

- A homemade layer cake looks professional if decorated well. Place a couple of mini calla lilies on the top layer, then stagger one on each tier, bending the stems around so that they conform to the shape of the cake. Other easy but beautiful choices for decorating are candied flowers, or fresh fruits such as raspberries or chocolate-dipped strawberries.

NATALIE'S DREAM CREAM CHEESE ICING

4 oz real butter
1 lb real cream cheese
2 lbs icing sugar
1 tsp vanilla
2 tbsp milk, if needed

In a medium bowl, beat butter and cream cheese together until smooth. Gradually add sugar. Beat on high until smooth (about 1 minute). Thin with milk to ice cake smoothly; use at full strength for piping borders.

CHAPTER ONE

Natalie Thompson felt a little woozy. In fact, she felt a lot woozy.

Wouldn't it be just ducky if the cake artist collapsed on top of a vastly expensive five-layer wedding cake?

"Not now, not now," she whispered desperately, blowing a strand of blond bangs out of her eyes. The chatter of wedding guests filing into the reception warned her to hurry.

Her fingers trembled as she made one last adjustment to the glittering cake topper. As a group of classy wedding planners, she and her best friends/coworkers, collectively known as the Wedding Belles, took pride in making other women's dreams come true. Right now *her* fondest dream was to remain upright for another ten minutes.

The air in front of her eyes danced with black spots. Ten minutes might be pushing it.

Why, oh why, hadn't she taken time to eat something? With all the activity of setting up for today's wedding, she'd used up every drop of sugar in her body. Now her insulin had kicked in, expecting to be balanced out with a meal.

Diabetes, the bane of her existence since she was seven, could be so unforgiving.

A mountain of sugar in front of her and she dare not snitch a bite lest she destroy the picture-perfect confection that had taken days to create. Not that she was supposed to eat sugar in the first place.

Breath a bit short, she stepped back to survey the table. This was the first Christmas wedding of the season and, in keeping with the holiday theme, the cake sat on a raised pedestal beneath a beribboned archway of twinkling silver, blue and white snowflake lights. Beneath them the cake's frosting glistened like new-fallen snow.

Draping the table in heavy white satin with wide blue bows and tiny silver bells tucked up at the corners had been Serena's latest creation, an idea the Belles' dress designer had brought back from the bridal show in Seattle. Natalie glanced around to find the cool, elegant blonde taking one last survey of the ballroom. Serena had also brought back something else from the bridal fair and subsequent plane crash that had scared them all to death. She'd brought back a rather wild and dangerous pilot, Kane Wiley, who had looked ready to eat her up like the last bite of creamy vanilla cheesecake.

Ah, yes. Cheesecake. Sugar. Food. Her job and her dilemma.

Everything was ready for the reception, right down to the fruit circling the dark-chocolate groom's cake. She'd spent hours dipping and decorating those strawberries to resemble tiny tuxedos. Nobody, not even her, was going to mess that up before the bride arrived. No matter how badly her knees wobbled.

"Natalie, are you okay? You look funny." The speaker was Regina O'Ryan, Natalie's good friend and the Wedding Belles' exceptionally gifted photographer. Though she always complained about her generous hips and extra ten pounds, Regina looked great these days. Glowing, happy, fulfilled. Marriage to her very own Mr. Right had done that for the lovely brunette.

People all around Natalie were falling in love faster than she could pipe leaves onto a birthday cake. Natalie was glad for them, especially Regina after all she'd been through. Truly she was. Love was great until

11

it let you down.

A too familiar pang of bitterness pinched the center of her chest. Right now was not the time to remember. It was also not the time to slither to the gleaming tiled floor like butter-cream frosting on a July day.

She waved Regina away. The action took more effort than she'd like.

"Insulin crash. No biggie." All Natalie's friends knew about her unpredictable diabetic condition and fretted appropriately. She appreciated it, really she did, but she and Regina were both too busy at the moment to deal with her temperamental endocrine system. "The bride and groom cometh. Better get moving."

Regina glanced in the direction of the arched doorway, and her soft brown eyes widened. "Eek. Can't miss the grand entrance." She pointed at the fruit display across the room. "Go eat something. Now."

Regina snapped one more shot of the bride's table and then hurried off, red heels clicking on white tile.

Eat something. Good advice. That's exactly what Natalie had to do.

Oh, for a mouthful of richly frosted, sweet buttery cake. But she'd long ago come to grips with the fact that she could have her cake but she couldn't eat it. Which was exactly why she was a cake artist, or cake fairy as she preferred to be called.

On the opposite side of the grand ballroom, rows and rows of fruit cascaded around a tiered table. Strawberries, grapes, melon, pineapple all beckoned. The table looked miles away, but fruit was one thing she could snitch without it being noticed. She edged in that direction, the wobble in her knees more pronounced. Usually careful about her diet, she'd been running late after the twins' babysitter had canceled at the last minute, a victim of the evil twenty-four-hour virus. With the scramble to get the girls dressed and driven to day care, she simply had not had time to think of food.

But, boy, was she thinking about it now. A cluster of big juicy green grapes practically screamed her name. Just as she reached for it, a male voice stopped her.

"Natalie!"

Like a kid caught stealing candy, she yanked her hand away and spun around. The room tilted.

"Hey." A pair of powerful hands gripped her upper arms. "Steady, there. Are you okay? Am I that much of a surprise?"

Surprise? What was he talking about? She blinked up at the expensive-smelling guest. He was tall, but then everyone was tall in her world. At just under five feet, she was vertically challenged. The only people shorter were her eight-year-old daughters.

"Natalie?" The man's voice reminded her of someone, but she was zoning out. She hated zoning out, but that was the price she sometimes paid when her sugar levels plummeted. And were they ever plummeting! Any minute now she'd slide to the floor and make a spectacle of herself.

"Fruit," she whispered, knowing she'd feel like an idiot later, but right now she had to have food. "Diabetes."

The stranger didn't hesitate. With rapid efficiency, he slid two pieces of the sweetest, most heavenly melon between her lips. Then, arm around her waist, he guided her onto a chair against the wall. If she hadn't felt so awful, she might have enjoyed having a man take such good care of her again.

Well, on second thought, maybe not. The one thing in her life she'd sworn never to do again was depend on anyone, especially a man, to take care of her. Once bitten, twice shy, as they say. Not that Justin hadn't loved her. That was the problem. He'd loved her too much. So much that she'd depended on him for every single thing.

A stab of loss penetrated the fog of diabetes.

"I'd forgotten you're a diabetic," the deep gentle voice rumbled as he poked more fruit into her mouth. The brush of manly fingers against her lips would have been erotic in another setting.

He'd forgotten? Who was this guy?

She tried to look at him, but her eyes wouldn't open.

She chewed and swallowed, chewed and swallowed, grateful to whomever he was.

In the background, the reception was in full swing, the sound muffled by the roaring in her head. The DJ announced the first dance, and a sexy version of "Let's Get It On" filled the air.

Natalie thought it an odd choice for the first dance. If she were the one getting married, she'd have chosen something sentimental and romantic. But then, she was never getting married again. Mr. Right came along only once if a girl was really lucky. She'd had her chance and look how that had turned out.

"Natalie," her rescuer said, tapping at her lips. "One more bite."

Like an obedient bird, she opened her mouth. Her heart wasn't racing quite as fast now and her head had begun to clear.

The fructose was doing its job.

She raised her eyelids, blinked them clear.

Concerned eyes as warm and rich as chocolate ganache stared back. Familiar eyes. Familiar face. Dressed in a dark suit, he crouched in front of her, one hand balancing a plate of fruit on a muscular thigh.

Natalie's heart thumped once, hard.

"Cooper?" she gasped. "What are you doing here? Is that really you?"

Dr. Cooper Sullivan flashed the wide, sexy grin that had stolen the hearts of any number of coeds in college. "It was me a few minutes ago when I looked in the mirror."

"But you're in California." She sat up straight, shaking the cobwebs out of her head.

Cooper looked around, mouth quirked. "I am?"

"Well, you're obviously here, but I mean . . ." She was making a total idiot of herself. That's what she'd meant. But then, she could always blame the sugar drop. The truth was, she hadn't seen the man in years, but articulating that sentiment didn't seem possible at the moment.

Cooper let her off the hook. "Right now I'm attending a colleague's wedding. Mutual friends, perhaps?"

"No, no. Clients. I'm working." She nodded toward the bride's table where a gor-

16

geous redhead in ice-blue satin served wedding cake to a parade of guests. "Only, I should have been gone by now. The cake fairy does her job and gets out of the way. Usually."

One of Cooper's dark, slashing eyebrows hiked. "Cake fairy?"

She nodded, gaining strength and clarity by the moment. No matter how long she dealt with diabetes, she was always amazed at how quickly she could crash and recover. "I design cakes for a local wedding planner, the Wedding Belles."

She was good at it, too. She could turn any idea into a fabulous cake. Justin had laughed when she'd taken up cake design but she thanked God every day she had. Otherwise, she and the twins would be sponging off relatives. She shivered at the thought. Even now finances were incredibly tight.

"Feeling better?" Cooper pushed to his feet and towered over her.

"I am. Thanks." Emitting a shaky breath, she ran a hand across her forehead. "I know better than to scrimp on lunch. But sometimes I can slide by."

"Not today. You were as white as the bride's dress." He sat down in the chair next to her as though he was in no hurry to join

17

the rest of the wedding guests. "Does Justin know about these episodes?"

Misery swept through her. He didn't know. Cooper Sullivan had been Justin's friend and closest competitor all through college and medical school but they'd gone their separate ways after graduation. Actually, after Justin and Natalie married. More than ten years had passed since she'd last seen the darkly handsome doctor. A lot can happen in ten years.

"Oh, Cooper." Natalie reached for his hand to soften the coming blow. "Justin died."

As a medical doctor, he must have said or heard those words dozens of times, but he jerked back, shocked. "Died? How? When? Natalie, no."

Even after all this time, the grief could sometimes slam into her like a shark attack, fierce, sharp, tearing. When it did, she replaced the pain with anger. If he'd had any sense, if he'd loved her and the twins enough, Justin would still be here.

"Two years ago. A motorcycle accident."

No use going into the horrifying details. When a motorcycle takes on an eighteen-wheeler, the motorcycle loses every time.

"God," he said and leaned back against the wall to run both hands through the sides of stylishly groomed black hair. "Nat, I am so sorry. Are you okay? You should have called me."

She didn't bring up the fact that he had been the one to fade out of their lives when he'd moved to California to accept a residency training program at USC. She also didn't mention the competition between him and Justin, a competition that had extended from the classroom to the sporting arena and finally to a bid for her affections. When she'd chosen Justin, their friendship had died out. Natalie was smart enough to realize it had never been her whom Cooper had wanted. His real desire had been the thrill of victory.

"The girls and I are fine, Cooper. It's been hard, losing Justin, making a life without him, but we're managing." In truth, she was barely staying afloat.

"The girls?" Still shocked, his handsome face registered bewilderment.

He had no way of knowing Justin had left her with the most amazing daughters. Without them to care for, she might have given in to the awful grief and simply disappeared.

"Twins. Rose and Lily. They're eight now."

"Twins. Amazing." He shook his head, soft smile pensive. "Old Justin has two little girls. I'd like to meet them."

Natalie carefully sidestepped the subtle hint. "What about you? What are you doing back in Boston after all this time?"

White teeth flashed against a Southern California tan. "All that sunshine and warm weather grew tiresome. I yearned for a good old Massachusetts nor'easter. Snow, wind, frigid air."

"No, seriously." She turned in her seat, picked a grape from the plate, and popped it into her mouth. "Are you only here for the wedding? Visiting friends? Or maybe someone special?"

Had that sounded too . . . interested? She hoped not. She didn't care one whit if Dr. Cooper Sullivan had twenty women on the string. Which he probably did. For Cooper, women, like everything else, were a prize to be won, a competition. Once he claimed the trophy, he quickly grew bored and moved on. Medicine and success were the only lovers that could hold him for long.

"Not visiting, though my family lives in the area." He reached for a strawberry. "I'm back to stay."

Oh, yes. How could she have forgotten that Cooper was one of *the* Sullivans, one of Massachusetts's prominent political families? "They must be thrilled to have you closer to home. Where will you be practicing?"

At the mention of his family, something curious flickered in Cooper's brown eyes but he said, "I've joined a surgical team at Children's. Top-notch group with a great rep."

Of course they were. Children's was a fabulous facility. "Congratulations."

No doubt he was the top recruit and they'd paid him a fat bonus to join their team. Cooper had been the number-one student in the entire medical school, something that had driven Justin crazy. Cooper was always one or two points ahead of his strongest competitor, her late husband. She knew without asking that he'd enjoyed the same success in his residency program and subsequent practice.

Dr. Cooper Sullivan was the single most brilliant human being she'd ever met. In fact, there was nothing he couldn't succeed at if he tried. It was as if he had golden boy encoded on his DNA. The only problem with Cooper was his attitude. He expected to win. He expected to be the top and he didn't back off until he was. The same attitude extended to his love life. She wondered if he'd ever dated a woman because he liked her rather than viewing her as trophy for his shelf. She'd known Justin loved her for herself. Cooper had seen her as a challenge, a Mount Everest to conquer. Cooper Sullivan was not her kind of man. That is, if she was looking for a man, which she most assuredly was not.

By now the wedding guests crowded the dance floor, moving to the energy of a fast track. Belle Mackenzie, the matronly blond owner of the Wedding Belles and Natalie's boss, floated amongst them, occasionally speaking into her headset as she made sure every detail of the wedding went off without a hitch. Belle's warm, Southern style and true love of people was what made the Wedding Belles a success. Not a woman to miss anything, she was certain to have noticed that her cake designer was paying an inordinate amount of attention to a darkly handsome guest.

"I really should be going now." Natalie stood, glad her knees were no longer made of wet noodles.

He caught her hand. "Dance with me first."

She pulled back. "I'm not a guest."

He grinned. "I am."

Before she could protest further, he swept her into his arms and onto the dance floor. For a nanosecond, annoyance ruffled her feathers. The arrogant man never considered that she might not want to dance with him. To his way of thinking, every woman longed to be in the arms of Dr. Cooper Sullivan.

But Natalie swallowed her protest and went along with the dance. After all, he was Justin's long ago friend and, as much as she hated needing help, he'd been there for her today. His quick reaction had probably kept her from fainting and disrupting a very nice wedding. Even though Boston was his home city, he'd been gone a long time. Perhaps, he'd been relieved to find a familiar face among the new acquaintances. The least she could do was dance with the man.

She loved to dance, had been on the dance squad in high school, and had taken jazz and tap for years. Justin had promised to learn ballroom dance with her as soon as his residency was completed. She was still furious with him for having procrastinated about the lessons, just as he'd procrastinated about most things, including taking out life insurance.

One thing Justin hadn't put off was spending. If he or she had wanted something, no matter how expensive, he'd charged it. According to Justin, all residents lived on credit, knowing they would soon be making tons of money. She'd believed him. As a result, she was still paying off the mountain of debt, one month at a time.

"This is a nice surprise," Cooper muttered as he gazed down at her with his "I'm hot" smile.

She supposed he was. Okay, he really, really was. Dark, dark hair, black spiky lashes that drew attention to brilliant eyes and a proud, sculpted face would make any movie star jealous. He looked like a model or something.

He danced pretty well, too, if she'd admit it, moving with a fluid, confident rhythm as he guided her effortlessly around the floor.

On the first whirl, he held her at arm's length and made small talk. On the second whirl, he pulled her against his chest, trapping her hand in his. Natalie couldn't help breathing in the clean, crisp, woodsy essence of him. The wool of his jacket rubbed tantalizingly against her cheek. She hadn't been in a man's arms in a very long time, and she'd always loved the wonderful differences between the male and female physiques. Hard to soft. Strong to delicate. Big to petite. Later she'd remind herself of all the reasons why she was permanently off the male species.

When the music ended she tried to step back. Cooper held on. She raised her eyes to his, saw a challenge there.

"No need to rush off. It's been a long time. We have a lot of catching up to do."

Natalie glanced around the crowded dance floor where she spotted Belle chatting up the mother of the groom. Her boss lifted a wineglass in her direction along with a finely penciled eyebrow. Lovely. Now Belle would be asking questions about the handsome hunk with whom Natalie had been dancing. Belle was a die-hard romantic, a natural inclination given her business of coordinating the most beautiful weddings in New England.

She was also one of the greatest Southern ladies of all time. Belle Mackenzie had given Natalie this job, encouraged her to stand strong when the storms of life had nearly swept her under, and had been a motherly shoulder to cry on in times of distress. Natalie adored Belle, so much so that she wanted to live the rest of her life as Belle did, as an independent woman in charge of her own life. No man need apply. There was no opening for romance at the Thompson house.

"I'm supposed to be working," she said.

Still, Cooper made no move to release her hand. She gave a gentle tug. He held fast, an enigmatic smile tilting those aristocratic lips.

"Nothing for you to do." He nodded toward the bride's table before smoothly sweeping Natalie back into his arms.

Blame it on the insulin reaction, blame it on the romantic swirl of bridal lace and the clink of champagne glasses, but Natalie could no more resist dancing with Cooper than she could conduct the Boston Pops.

After all, what he'd said was true enough. Her glorious creation was being whittled to nothing as guests came back for seconds, murmuring over its deliciousness. There wasn't anything for Natalie to do until the reception ended except enjoy the compliments.

Cooper's strong fingers clasped her much smaller hand against his chest. She felt the rhythmic beat of his heart, noticed the hard contours of his athletic torso. Though she tried not to think of Cooper as an attractive man, with the number of interested female glances coming his way as a constant reminder, she was failing miserably. She resented the feelings. Resented the reminders that she was a passionate woman alone. Especially she didn't like the idea of betraying Justin's memory with his once close competitor.

"Tell me about your new job," she said, frantic not to notice Cooper's muscular thighs brushing hers or the tingle of awareness that rushed from her own thighs upward.

He gave her a lazy smile. "I'm boring. Tell me about you."

Boring? She doubted there was anything boring in Cooper's life.

She, on the other hand, was quite ordinary and content to be so. A Friday-night poker game with the other Wedding Belles, a little gossip, Sunday afternoons in the park with her kids.

"Working. Taking care of my girls. Not much else."

"And the cakes?"

"Oh, yes. Lots and lots of cakes."

"Sweet," he said and they both laughed.

"How, or perhaps I should ask why, did a diabetic choose to be a cake decorator?"

"Fairy," she corrected.

"Ah, yes. Cake fairy." His eyes twinkled. "It suits you."

"My girls think I should wear a Tinkerbell costume with wings and a tutu."

A wicked gleam. "Now *that* I'd like to see."

"I've actually thought about it. For kids' birthday parties, I mean. They would love it."

He laughed down at her and something low in her belly reacted. She hadn't felt this way in more than two years. Feminine, attractive, womanly.

The shock of it caused her to misstep.

"Sorry," she said as a blush warmed her neck and cheeks. Hopefully, Cooper would blame the stumble for her sudden fluster.

"No problem. You need to rest anyway after that insulin reaction. I shouldn't have kept you out here so long."

As if reluctant to break contact, he held on to her hand and led her toward a white linen-clad table. Still stunned at her unexpected reaction to his very male nearness, Natalie followed without resistance.

"Something to drink?" he asked.

As she sank into a chair, she nodded. "Water would be great. I'm hot."

Cooper inclined his head with a wicked smile. "I'd have to agree."

Her flushed skin grew redder. How long had it been since she'd even thought of herself as an attractive woman? As a hot babe?

"Go away, Cooper," she teased, trying to laugh off her sudden discomfiture.

He laughed, too, but did as she said, returning in a very short amount of time with their drinks. "I wanted to try your cake but it's all gone."

"Even the groom's cake?"

"Every crumb. You must be a great cake fairy."

Before she could think of a witty comeback, Cooper's cell phone chirped.

"Excuse me," he said as he reached inside his jacket and drew out the instrument. "Dr. Sullivan."

An amazing transformation happened before her eyes. She'd seen it with Justin. Cooper's face, animated, teasing and maybe a tad flirty a moment ago became a study in serious listening. The brilliant mind behind the playboy smile kicked into high gear.

"Call Dr. Francis. Ask him to assist. I'll meet him there in twenty minutes."

He snapped the phone shut and slid it inside his jacket.

"A patient?" Natalie asked.

He nodded and pushed back from the table. "Sorry to break up the party. It's been great seeing you again, Natalie."

Natalie experienced a frisson of disappointment. "It was good to see you too, Cooper. I hope all goes well with your patient."

He tilted his head, whipped around to leave but turned back just as quickly to

29

hand her a business card. "Call me. We'll get together."

With that he was gone, straight back and wide shoulders slicing through the crowd with a confident air until she lost sight of him.

She gazed down at the card bearing his address and phone number in a bold confident font.

Call him? Call a man who'd rattled her self-imposed moratorium on male-female relationships?

Not likely.

CHAPTER TWO

"Good case, Dr. Sullivan."

Seated on a narrow chair in the doctors' lounge, Cooper lifted one foot to remove the protective shoe coverings. The scent of coffee, too long on the burner, filled his nostrils. His stomach growled but the stale doughnuts on the sideboard held no charm.

He peeled off the blue shoe cover and tossed it into the trash before nodding to the dark-haired female. "Yes, it was. Thanks for your help."

"A pleasure." Dr. Genevieve Pennington was a member of Children's Cardiac Surgical and as such one of his associates. She was also a skilled surgeon as cool under pressure as he. Now she tarried in the doorway of the physicians' lounge, fiddling with the clasp on a green alligator handbag.

"Some of us are headed to the country club for a drink. Care to join us?"

Cooper glanced up at the attractive doctor, wondering if the invitation was business, pleasure or both. Never mind. He was tired and feeling strangely let down though he couldn't say why. He loved his work and the surgery had gone better than expected. Normally he enjoyed an active social life, as well, and Dr. Pennington was single, attractive and smart. In the weeks since he'd joined the practice, she'd dropped other subtle hints that he couldn't miss. They had plenty in common, but he wasn't sure a fling with a colleague would benefit either of them in the long run.

He shook his head. "Rain check?"

Disappointment flickered briefly on the doctor's face. "Sure." She backed out of the lounge, one hand on the door handle. "See you tomorrow."

"Right — 6:00 a.m. atrial-septal defect. I'll pop up and say hello to the patient and his mother before I head home."

Home. A town house in East Cambridge. Beautiful, well appointed, empty.

Cooper blew out a tired and somewhat depressed sigh. He didn't really want to go home. Maybe he'd drive out to see his parents. Or maybe not. He wasn't up to facing Dad's dissatisfaction today. Oh, the old man never came right out and said anything, but he'd made his feelings clear. Cooper hadn't followed his father's lead. He hadn't gone to Harvard. He'd chosen medicine instead of politics. Everyone knew the blue-blooded Sullivans were shoo-ins for public office, and with Cooper's charisma he could have risen to the top. Or so his family thought.

He'd never managed to convince his father that he wasn't cut out to hobnob with people he disliked, and he wasn't much on kissing babies. He just wanted to save their lives.

Cooper rubbed a hand over the back of his neck, tense from the five-hour surgery, tenser still from the ongoing knowledge that he'd let his parents down. He'd thought coming back to Boston might help ease the constant feeling of discontent, the need to reach higher and higher, but if anything, being near his family had made it worse.

Quiet settled over the usually busy lounge.

For years he'd strived to be here in this place with these physicians doing this work. All afternoon he'd battled death and won, giving a future to a four-year-old with malformed heart valves. In another place or time the boy would never have lived to adolescence. Now he'd be an old man with grandchildren on his knees.

This was what Cooper wanted out of life.

This kind of success. Yet it felt empty.

In a few years, if he worked hard and remained focused, he would be chief of cardiac surgery. Perhaps then he'd experience the sense of satisfaction that always remained just out of reach.

Rolling his head to loosen the kinks, he stretched upward and went to his locker. The day's personal mail, picked up earlier from the office was stuffed inside, unopened. Flipping through the stack, two caught his eye. His pulse accelerated. Could it be?

He took the innocuous-looking envelopes to a chair and sat down again to slide a finger beneath the flap and remove the letter. As he read, the depression of moments before sailed away. He scanned faster, coming to the final conclusion. They wanted him.

"All right!" he exclaimed.

Growing more energized with every minute, he ripped open the other envelope. After another quick scan, he pumped a fist in victory. "Yes. Yes. Yes!"

He was tempted to jump up and do a happy dance around the empty lounge. This little trick could put him on the map as one of the premier neonatal surgeons on the planet.

Several months ago — he'd forgotten how many — he'd submitted his research and findings on a technique he'd perfected that helped protect a newborn's still developing brain from damage during a cardio-pulmonary bypass. The science was good. The technique precise. The results stunning.

Now, he held not one, but two letters asking to publish his findings. Both the *American Journal of Medicine* and the *British Lancet,* two of the most prestigious medical journals in the world, wanted the article. The news would put his name on the lips of every pediatric surgeon and elevate his status among the powers that be here in Boston. He wanted to be one of the youngest chiefs ever, and the goal grew closer with every breath.

This wasn't his first publication, but it was the most important. The drive to perfect surgical techniques in newborns was like a living thing inside him. The fate of tiny little human beings with all their lives spread out before them rested in his hands and inside his brain.

The more he studied, the more he tweaked medications and methods, the more lives he saved. These acceptances were more motivation to burn the midnight oil. Who needed rest when so much was at stake?

Needing someone to share his excitement, he whipped out his cell phone and punched in his father's number. The congressman would be proud of this.

"Cooper?" Randall Sullivan's voice, strong and confident boomed into his earpiece. "Is that you?"

"Yes, sir. How are you and mother doing?" Get the niceties out of the way first.

"Hale and hearty. Busy as the devil himself."

"I won't keep you long, but I did have something to tell you." A zing of adrenaline had him tapping his foot.

"Hold on a minute, son. I've got another call. Governor Bryson's office." A click and then silence. Cooper stared down at the letter, rereading the good news while he waited.

Another click and then his father's voice again, robust and oratorical even to family. "Still there?"

"I'm here, Dad." He leaned forward, elbows on knees, the acceptance letter dangling in front of his eyes.

"Good. I was about to call you with the news. Cameron's decided to make a run for state office. The party thinks he has a good chance. Youth, looks, charisma."

"With the Sullivan machine behind him?"

Congressman Sullivan's laugh boomed. "Absolutely."

Cooper's younger brother had followed the rules of the Sullivan household and gone into law with an eye to politics. Cameron was now viewed as the good son. Not that Cooper was complaining. Cameron's natural propensity for their father's profession took some of the pressure off Cooper. Some, but not all.

Congressman Randall Sullivan dreamed of creating a political dynasty to rival the Kennedy clan. The trouble was his elder son had not cooperated, and this had caused more than a little tension within the family.

"Cam's still young, Dad. He needs to be certain this is what he wants."

"Jack Kennedy was in the Oval Office at forty-three. A man has to make his move when the climate is right. That's politics. If you had stayed the course, you'd be in the Senate by now."

The censure was there, subtle, but sharp like a sticker in a sock.

"Dad," he said simply, not wanting to revisit this old wound.

"This is what you were born for, Cooper, what your mother and I reared you to do with your life. The Sullivans are public servants. It's our responsibility to care for those less fortunate. There's still time for you to throw your hat in the ring. I know the party would be interested. Two Sullivan brothers running for office this election year would make great press and garner big voter turnout."

Cooper bit back his usual argument. Putting broken hearts back together *was* public service. Sure he was paid well, but so was the congressman.

"I'm a doctor." He glanced at the letter, wanting to say that he wasn't just a doctor, he was a good doctor, a surgeon moving up through the ranks at a rapid pace. But the senator was only interested in one game, and it wasn't medicine.

His fingers tightened on the acceptance letter, euphoria seeping out like a leaking oxygen tank.

"A good strategist can use the doctor angle," his father was saying. "The surgeon who comes to politics to heal society's wounds. Something like that. What do you say?"

"I don't think so, Dad. I'm —"

"Don't say no yet. Think about it. That's all I'm asking. Think about it."

Trying to talk to his father was like spitting into the wind. He was always the one who was sorry.

"Okay, son? You'll do that for the old man, won't you? Think about it?"

Cooper swallowed against the tightness in his throat. This was why his father was one of the most influential men in the state. He knew how to get what he wanted. "I'm sorry, Dad."

Truly, he was sorry. Sorry to be a disappointment. Sorry he couldn't be what his father needed and wanted him to be.

The silence that extended from his father's line to his buzzed for several painful seconds before the congressman cleared his throat. When he spoke, his voice was tight with disapproval.

"We've got our first fund-raiser for your brother scheduled on the thirtieth. I hope you can find it in your busy schedule to be there."

Cooper didn't miss the subtle jab. "I'll be there. Tell Cam to let me know if I can help in any other way." Short of running with him.

"Will do. Now, wasn't there something you wanted to talk to me about?"

Cooper glanced once more at the letter, crumpled in one corner by his ever-tightening fingers. The joy he'd wanted to share with someone close was so far gone he couldn't even remember what it had felt like. "Nothing important."

"All right then. You'll have to excuse me. I have a meeting to attend. Senator Steiner thinks he can sway my vote on that worthless bridge project of his." He chuckled roughly. "Maybe I'll let him if he makes all the right noises about helping Cameron. Come for dinner on Sunday. Make your mother happy."

It was more of a command than an invitation. "I'll be there. Thank you, sir."

As deflated as a child's balloon, he flipped his cell phone closed and stared at the crisscross pattern in the tile floor. He shouldn't let his father get to him, but he always did.

It would be different when he made chief. The congressman would see far more advantage in a position of prominence than just being a member of the team. No matter how prestigious the group, according to his father, Sullivans weren't team members. They were the head man. Anything less was not acceptable.

In a fit of frustration, Cooper wadded the letter into a ball, aimed it toward the trash can and, with a flip of his wrist, arched the paper like a miniature basketball. The white vellum hit its mark. Cooper's mouth turned up in a self-deprecating grin.

"Two points," he murmured.

The action reminded him of his old buddy and one-on-one opponent, Justin Thompson. They must have shot a million paper wads during medical school, and they'd bet on every single one. Right now, he'd give a year of his life to see his former friend. Even though Justin would be green with jealousy over the journal acceptances, he would also be happy for Cooper's success. That was the fuel that drove their friendship — fierce competition coupled with a deep respect and affection. If he couldn't win, he wanted Justin to take first place. He knew Justin had felt the same.

His foot dropped to the floor with a thud. He stared at the wall. Justin was dead. Unbelievable.

The shock still stung like an injection of xylocaine. One of the brightest guys he'd ever encountered, gone. A good man, a great competitor, a true friend.

A motorcycle wreck. He shuddered at the thought. But that was Justin. A man who pushed the envelope, ready to take chances, to try new and exciting things. It was what had made their friendship so exhilarating at times. He'd never known what Justin would do next.

Regret pulled at him. They hadn't parted on the best of terms. His fault, he was sure.

But he should have kept in touch, should have called, should at least have known a friend had died before his time. A physician of all people knew how frail life could be.

Two young doctors entered the lounge, both yawning with the exhaustion common to overworked residents but bantering with the black humor that kept them awake and alert for thirty-plus hours.

He and Justin had done that, although their jokes had always been competitive, each trying to outdo the other.

Funny how he hadn't thought about that in a long time, but now the camaraderie came back with the clarity of HDTV.

An ache pulled at his gut. He missed that kind of friendship.

As he skimmed into his street clothes, his mind strayed to the sprite of a woman Justin had left behind. Encountering Natalie at Dr. Craggin's wedding had been a surprise. A pleasant one. When he'd seen her across the room, he'd done a double take. Ten years ago, she'd been a cute girl, but now she was a woman, all grown-up and looking good. Real good. He felt a little guilty about thinking of her in those terms, but there it was.

When they'd danced and her taut little body had brushed against his, he'd suffered a flash of desire so hot, he'd thought the building was on fire. After finding out about Justin's death, he'd also had an overwhelming need to take care of her, as if by doing so he could make up for the loss he hadn't known about.

The knowledge made him itchy, uncomfortable. He didn't know what was wrong with him to have such crazy thoughts.

Even after he'd finished the emergency surgery that night, she'd been on his mind. Her soft mouth around his fingers as he'd fed her fruit had just about done him in. Later, when his mind had kept replaying the scene without his permission, the moment had taken flight into erotic fantasy. Honey dew. Even the melon was sexy. He should be ashamed of himself.

Wasn't it wrong to think of his friends' wife this way, even when that friend was dead? *Especially* when that friend was dead? Justin wasn't here to protect what was his.

There was that word again — *protect.*

Maybe that was it. Maybe Justin would expect him to look after his woman. Like a friend or a brother, not as a lusting fool who only had one thing in mind.

Ten years ago Natalie's big blue eyes had been guileless and even a little gullible. Now they were wary and wise. Though common

43

sense said the death of a spouse would change anyone, the difference bothered him. Just as he'd been bothered when Justin had won her affections.

His hands stilled on his silk tie as the notion caught him up short. That was years ago. A college crush. Both men vying for the blond pom-pom girl with the flashing dimples and sexy legs. Justin had won. Subject closed.

To him she'd been a passing fancy, but Justin had been the family type. He had wanted it all — career, family, adventure, success — and that had been enough reason for Cooper to back off. Justin had thought he could juggle everything. Cooper knew better. Single-minded focus was the only way to reach a lofty goal. Justin's death only proved how right he'd been. A man couldn't have it all, at least not for long.

He slipped into a pair of Italian loafers.

Natalie still had those flashing dimples.

She had two little girls, too. Justin's girls. Far better to focus on them. Were they doing all right? Did they need anything? It wouldn't hurt to make certain Justin had left them well provided for.

He'd asked Natalie to call. Wonder why she hadn't?

Once again he pulled his cell phone from

his jacket, but then sat down, staring at it. He didn't know her number.

Then he smiled. He wasn't Congressman Randall Sullivan's son for nothing.

"Lily, get down from there. You're going to fall."

At least Natalie *thought* it was Lily walking tight rope on the back of the couch. With identical twins, even she couldn't always tell them apart from a distance.

Cradling the phone between her shoulder and ear, she blended confectioner's sugar and real butter with almond extract using a mixer that had seen better days. "Listen, Regina, I've got to go. The timer is going off and Lily has suddenly decided to become a high rope circus act."

"Call me later. I'm dying to hear more about that dreamy doctor."

"Regina," Natalie warned, but a little thrill jitterbugged up and down her nerve endings. "Cooper is just a former friend who recognized the insulin reaction. End of story. I don't know why I told you in the first place."

Thank goodness she hadn't mentioned the crazy dreams she'd had since then, confusing dreams of being held and loved and cherished by a man with very dark eyes and long, slender hands.

Regina's warm chuckle was knowing. "Just promise to tell me more later. You tell me something, and I'll tell you something. A tit for tat, as it were."

"Okay, whatever." Natalie laughed and rang off, clapped the phone onto the counter and whirled toward the beeping oven, grabbing a potholder as she moved. The duplex was so small the kitchen, living and dining room were blended together in one big area. Most of the space was taken up with her tables and equipment. Fortunately, she could work and still keep a close eye on her active girls.

As she slid the sheet cake from the oven, she heard her daughter give a tiny sigh of exasperation and then heard the thud of feet as the child hopped onto the wood floor. It was Lily, all right. Rose wouldn't have given in so easily.

Natalie slid the cake onto a table and turned to look at the bouncy eight-year-old. Love as big and warm as a hot air balloon filled her chest.

"Rose won't play with me," Lily said, bottom lip extended, elfin face droopy.

"Yes, she will, punkie. Go ask her."

Big gray eyes, reminiscent of Justin's, gazed sadly at Natalie. "She won't. She says

46

Puppy doesn't like me today so I can't come in the room."

"Rose!" Natalie yelled, trying to be louder than the television cartoons. Rose had an imaginary dog that didn't like much of anyone except Rose. Whenever she was in a mood, she claimed Puppy would bite anyone who came into her bedroom — a room that also belonged to her sister.

Of her twins, Lily was the quieter, the more docile child, though sometimes when the two girls were together they could both be a handful.

The other twin, wearing a backward baseball cap and lime-green frog slippers appeared in the hallway. "Are we going to get a Christmas tree? Ashley already has one with ten presents under it."

Natalie ignored the obvious distraction technique. Rose was an expert at distraction. Natalie crossed the room to lower the volume on the TV set. "Play nicely with your sister or Santa might not bring you anything at all this year. No need for a tree in that case."

Rose perched a hand on one hip. "Mom! There is no Santa Claus."

Lily piped up at that. "Yes, there is. I saw him. Remember?"

Rose shot her sister a look. She might only

be two minutes older, but sometimes she behaved as though Lily was two. "That was Daddy. Santa doesn't come anymore since Daddy died."

Natalie's heart twisted right in half. Justin had dressed up in a Santa suit every year after the twins were born. He got such a kick out of their squealing reactions and out of making out with Mrs. Claus after the girls were fast asleep. But she couldn't for the life of her imagine how Rose could remember all that.

She went down on her knees in front of her daughter and pulled her close with one hand as she reached for Lily with the other. "Santa came last year. You just didn't see him."

"You don't have to pretend anymore, Mom," Rose said, far too grown-up for Natalie's comfort. "The presents are from you and Grandma in Arizona. I can tell. Santa always brought big stuff."

Oh, yes, Justin bought out the local toystore every year. "Well, big or not, lady, we always have Christmas."

"It's not about the stuff, anyway, is it, Mommy?" Lily, the peacemaker spoke up.

"No, sweetie, Christmas is not about the stuff." Though Justin had spoiled both her and the girls, Natalie had tried hard to teach them the real meaning of Christmas. Money may be tight now, but she wanted them to know how blessed they were. "Which reminds me. The three of us need to decide our Christmas project for this year. Shall we save pennies for the Salvation Army bell ringers? Pick an angel from the angel tree? Bake cakes for the homeless shelter? Your choice."

Rose and Lily screwed their identical faces into expressions of deep thought.

Finally, Lily asked, "If we bake cakes, will you let us help?"

The question took Natalie aback. Let them help? Two monkeys in her kitchen? "I don't know, girls. Let me give it some thought."

"We'll be real careful. We won't stick our fingers in the icing or anything."

"Or lick the spoon," Lily put in.

"Or nothing gross like that. We're not little kids anymore."

Natalie suppressed a smile. She had to love their independent spirits. She of all people should understand what it felt like to be told she couldn't do something. Justin had never wanted her to work, never thought she could handle the pressure of doing anything because of her diabetes. In his macho, overprotective way, he'd stolen her independence. She'd felt loved instead of insulted, but after his death, she'd only felt helpless.

"You know, I think you girls are right."

The twins exchanged wide-eyed glances. "We are?"

"Uh-huh. But you will have to promise not to touch anything that I'm working on for the business. Deal?"

They both nodded solemnly, saying in unison. "Deal."

"High-fives all around?"

The three slapped high-fives before Natalie grabbed them into a bear hug, tumbling onto the floor for a shower of kisses. Lord, how she loved her babies.

The timer went off again and she untangled herself from the pile of arms and legs to answer the call. She had tester cakes to bake for several brides with appointments at Belle's on Monday and a cake to decorate for a baby shower tomorrow.

Suddenly friends again, the twins dashed off to make Christmas plans while she got busy. Multitasking was her middle name. Two cakes in the ancient oven, another in progress on the counter, clothes in a basket to be folded and lunch still to be prepared. Her day never ended, but she could deal with that. At least she was making her own way, not being a pretty parasite on a man's arm.

As she shut the dishwasher with her foot while adding food coloring to six different bowls of frosting, Lily let out a yelp just as the doorbell chimed. Natalie jumped, splattering red down the front of her sweater onto the top of her foot.

The doorbell *ding-donged* again.

Rose streaked into sight. "I'll get it, Mom."

"Don't open that door," she warned.

Too late. A blast of artic air sucked the warm, toasty fragrance of caramel pecan cheesecake out into the frigid Saturday afternoon.

"Rose!" she yelled, frustrated that her daughter could never remember to peek before opening. A serial killer would have no problem gaining entrance into this house.

She came around the row of tables piled with her baking tools just as Rose remembered her instructions and tried to shut the door again. A gloved hand shot out, palm up, to brace the door open.

A jolt of concern raced up Natalie's back. That was a man's hand. Black leather gloves. No fingerprints.

Rushing now to protect her child, she stumbled over the basket of clothes in the

51

living room and pitched forward, catching her hip on the coffee table.

"That'll leave a mark," a deep voice said.

She looked up to find Cooper Sullivan now inside her house, once again sliding an arm around her waist to lead her to a chair. She felt small and helpless and protected.

"This is starting to be a habit."

Natalie didn't like feeling helpless. Been there, done that.

"This is starting to be ridiculous," she said, scowling at Rose. "Shut that door, Rose Isabella, and go to your room."

The two names rolled off her tongue with ease. She'd said them far more times than Lily Alexandra.

Rose obeyed, her look of chagrin indicating she knew when to make an exit.

Natalie needed to rub her hip bone but not in front of Cooper. What was he doing here, anyway?

"Cooper," she said, through gritted teeth. "What a surprise."

A low rumble of laughter. "Maybe I should have called first."

"Maybe."

"I could leave."

"No, of course not. Don't be silly." It wasn't his fault her heart was beating too fast and she'd made a fool of herself in his

52

presence — again. "Take off your coat and have a seat. I'll be recovered in a moment."

She gave up and rubbed the smarting hip.

"You're going to have a bruise," he said as he slipped out of his coat and draped the long garment over the back of the couch. "Want me to have a look?"

Raising her eyes, she shot him a glare intended to melt iron. He laughed. "Maybe some ice instead?"

"I don't have the patience to sit still that long."

"Still the fidgety type?"

"My teachers called it hyperactive."

He chuckled again and she relaxed the slightest bit. Seeing Cooper brought back a lot of memories and not all of them were bad. In fact, most of them weren't bad. That was the biggest problem with having him show up at her house looking all handsome and manly. Well, that and the lovely dreams.

"How did you know where I live?"

He shrugged. "I called your boss."

"Belle would never give out my personal information to a stranger."

"She saw us dancing together at the Craggins' wedding."

"Oh." Belle had better not be playing matchmaker. She knew Natalie didn't date, hadn't even considered dating since Justin's death. Now that she was an independent woman, she planned to stay that way.

"Don't worry. I told her we were old friends." He tilted his head toward her. Melting snowflakes glistened in his black hair. "We are still friends, aren't we?"

Now she felt silly and downright inhospitable. "Of course we are. It's good to see you again."

Really. It was. If only she didn't have this bizarre chemical reaction every time he came near. At the Craggins' wedding, she'd blamed it on an insulin reaction, though she hadn't been able to get him off her mind even when her blood sugar was perfectly normal. Today she had no excuse at all. But she wanted an excuse because the alternative meant admitting that Cooper made her . . . feel things.

And she didn't want to . . . feel things.

The heavenly scent of caramel cake once more wafted through the house. Thank goodness.

"Excuse me a minute, Cooper. I have to check my cakes." She hopped up, maneuvering around the basket and toys.

Cooper followed her into the narrow kitchen, his masculine presence filling the room. Natalie tried not to notice. No male in her age range had ever been in this kitchen.

"Don't let me interrupt anything. I just came by to . . ." His voice drifted off as his gaze fell to her feet. "You're bleeding."

"I am?" She looked down at the red liquid sliding between her toes and started to giggle. "Doctor, that is not blood."

She grabbed a paper towel and wiped her foot clean. "See? All fine now. The miracle of being a mom. We can turn blood to food coloring."

"Thank goodness. I was beginning to wonder how you survive alone."

He'd meant it as a joke, so Natalie tried not to be offended, but the words were exactly the kind of thing Justin would have said. She was fragile, sickly, unable to take care of herself.

Tempted to ask why he'd tracked her down, Natalie instead said, "Would you like some coffee?"

"Sounds good if it's already made. Don't go to extra trouble."

"I always have coffee going on a cold day." She poured him a cup and handed it to him. "And soup in the crock pot."

There was something deliciously unsettling about having Cooper Sullivan in her kitchen. He gave her the willies, in a good way. Not that she was interested, but any woman would notice Cooper's looks and class and overt sexuality, especially a woman who had barely even thought about sex in two years.

"Smart mom." He sipped, eyes twinkling at her over the rim.

To settle her jitters, Natalie grabbed the bowl of frosting and got back to work. "I hope you don't mind but I have a cake to decorate. The customer's coming for it tonight at six."

"Can I help?"

The idea of pediatric surgeon Cooper Sullivan helping her decorate anything brought a giggle. "You can taste the icings for me."

Both eyebrows shot up hopefully. "As in more than one?"

"Uh-huh. Six or eight. I haven't decided yet. I'm creating as I go. My friend Julie is getting married and we're planning a big fancy bash. I'm creating something special just for her." She shoved a tasting spoon toward him. "Try this. Too sweet? Enough vanilla bean? Be honest now."

He took the spoon and nibbled, rolling the thick, creamy frosting around his mouth as he would a good sip of wine. After serious consideration, a stunning smile broke over his face. *Oh, my.* All her head alarms started going off. He was too hunky, too close, too *everything.*

"This is awesome," he said around that dazzling smile. "Julie, whoever she is, will love it."

It was only cake icing, something she made all the time, but his compliment thrilled her unduly. "Then try this other one."

"Let me clear my palate with coffee."

She widened her eyes at him and giggled. "By all means, clear the palate."

She shoved a second and then a third type of frosting in his direction. He made silly, witty, and astute comments, always asking for just one more teeny bite. Taste testing with Cooper was far more fun than the frequent tastings she forced upon the other Belles.

"You know what would be even better?" he said after the third opinion was issued.

"What? Orange peel? Lemon zest?"

His grin teased. "Cake. You could run a little cake under these frostings and let me try again. I promise to give a learned, if somewhat biased, opinion."

She'd forgotten what a fun guy Cooper could be, so different from his serious physician side. Her alarms stopped clanging. There was nothing threatening about an old friend having cake in her kitchen. She

57

needed to get over herself.

"Let him eat cake," she proclaimed dramatically and opened the holding bin to display rows and rows of tiny bite-size cakes. "These are fresh, made for brides to taste test next week. I always take extras for the other Belles."

"What kind of bells are we talking about here? Jingle bells? Church bells? And they eat cake?"

With a lifter, she scooped several cake bites onto a saucer. "My coworkers. We're called the Belles, as in Wedding Bells but with a Southern flair. The other girls serve as my official testers since I can't try the sweets myself."

"Brutal if you ask me, to be a cake maker who can't eat cake. Why didn't you become something less tempting?"

"Long story."

He shrugged a sweater-clad shoulder. "I have time."

"No surgery today? I thought surgeons worked day and night."

"Only by choice. The brutal days are in residency. Once in private practice we get to have lives. At least within reason."

For a minute the words stabbed like pinpricks. Justin had never made it this far. He'd never had time for a regular life. He'd worked such crazy hours and even when he could have been sleeping, he'd chosen to ride his motorcycle or play golf or sail. If he got three hours of sleep out of twenty-four, he considered himself rested. Now she knew how foolish that idea had been. He'd been running on three hours sleep the day he'd missed that stop sign.

"When Justin died, I needed a way to support myself and the twins so I started baking cakes."

"You never finished your degree?"

"No." Much to her regret, she'd quit college to take a minimum-wage job when she and Justin had first married. Then when his residency had begun, she'd gotten pregnant. When her diabetes had gone crazy and landed her on bed rest to save the twins, Justin had freaked out. She'd been scared, too, and wanted to stay home with her babies. "When the girls were two, I convinced Justin to let me take a cake decorating class."

"Convinced him?"

"Oh, he didn't mind if I had a hobby, but he worried about my health. Afraid I couldn't handle the load because of my sometimes unpredictable diabetes." She grimaced at the sad irony. "He'd be surprised at how wrong he was."

Cooper propped a hip on her kitchen counter and looked at her for a long moment. In a quiet voice he asked, "Have things been that difficult for you?"

The kindness in his tone rattled her. Normally she didn't share her worries with anyone but Regina or Belle. "A little."

"What about Justin's insurance?"

She scooted the saucer across the countertop.

"He didn't have any."

Cooper's long, talented fingers paused on an inch cube of Italian cream cake. "None?"

"He kept intending to get some. After he died I found an application on his desk." She shrugged one shoulder. It was all a moot point now.

"That sucks."

At the blunt and un-Cooperlike assessment, she smiled. "I think I may have said that a few million times in the past two years."

A beat of silence passed. Then Cooper reached across the narrow space between them and tilted her chin, meeting her gaze with his earnest one. "I'm really sorry, Nat. Justin was a good man. He wouldn't have done anything to purposely hurt you. He was crazy about you."

Tears prickled the backs of her eyelids.

She'd long since passed the point of un-quenchable grief, and most of the time she was just plain mad at Justin for having left her alone. But Cooper's compassion was both unexpected and touching.

"*Crazy* being the operative word," she murmured, trying to keep her mind *on* the conversation and off the warm strength of Cooper's fingers. Off the random thought that she could smell his cologne. Off the reminder that she'd once entertained ro-mantic thoughts about him.

Something shifted in the caramel-scented air. Cooper pushed away from the counter, eyes never leaving her face.

Her heart set up a thunder dance, and her mind raced like two hamsters on a Ferris wheel. What was he doing? Why was he moving toward her with that wild glint in his eyes? Was he going to hug her? Comfort her? Kiss her?

Before she could find out, a feral growl from somewhere behind them ripped through the kitchen.

CHAPTER THREE

Cooper whirled around at a sudden noise from behind him. A puck-faced child with teeth bared catapulted toward him, growling like a doberman.

"Rose!" Natalie stepped smoothly between him and the ponytailed stick of dynamite.

The little girl's eyes slanted in menace. "Puppy's going to bite him."

"Puppy is going back in your room right now if he can't behave himself. Dr. Sullivan is a guest and neither you nor Puppy is going to bite him." Natalie grabbed the child's hand and pulled her forward. "You owe Dr. Sullivan an apology."

When the child crossed her arms, chin tilted in a stubborn pose, Natalie crouched down in front of her. "*Now,* Rose."

At the firm tone, Rose huffed once and then capitulated.

"I'm sorry, Dr. Sullivan. Puppy won't bite you. He's just in a bad mood today."

"Is he always in a bad mood?" Cooper asked, trying to keep a straight face. The invisible puppy must be Rose's alter ego.

"Most of the time." She glanced down at the floor as if a real dog waited at her side. "It's okay, Puppy. He's not a criminal like you thought. He's a doctor."

Natalie made a strange noise in the back of her throat. When Cooper looked up in question, her eyes danced. "She's been warned against opening the front door without checking first to make sure it's someone I allow in the house."

"Ah, that explains it."

Natalie gave a wry shrug. "With Rose, we can never be too sure."

At that moment an identical child, minus the backward ball cap, entered the room.

Although she wasn't growling and didn't look nearly as menacing, Cooper asked, "Should I brace myself for another imaginary dog attack?"

"Puppy doesn't like me, either," the new addition said, tone dejected. "I wish we had a real dog that didn't bite."

"These," Natalie said, drawing the children towards him, "are my girls, Rose and Lily. Girls, meet Dr. Cooper Sullivan."

"Are you my mama's new boyfriend?" Rose asked, glaring at him with a look that said her dog was getting riled again.

The question took him aback. Natalie's boyfriend? Sweat broke out on the back of his neck. A man on the fast track in his profession didn't do relationships. Occasional dates, a night here and there, but not the boyfriend-girlfriend thing. No time for that kind of commitment.

"Rose! Will you please behave yourself? Cooper is a friend. We went to the same college."

Lily, conversely, came forward as polite as could be and extended her small hand. "Nice to meet you. Did you go to college with my daddy, too?"

"Yes, I did. And medical school, as well. Your dad was a friend of mine." A friend that should be here giving him a hard time.

This news seemed to win some points with Rose because she stepped up and extended her hand, albeit a bit grudgingly. "I'm Rose. That's Lily. We're twins."

"It must be fun to have a twin."

The peanut-size child jerked one shoulder. "Sometimes."

"Bet you try to fool people, too, don't you?"

Rose slanted a warning glance at her sister. Cooper swallowed a laugh. This one probably coerced her twin into monkey business all the time.

Natalie had moved away from the children to stand closer to him. He tried not to notice the curve of her lips or remember the feel of her warm, soft mouth on his fingers. That fantasy had a way of popping up at the most inopportune times as it had done just before Rose had interrupted. Thank goodness for the little girl. He'd almost made a tactical error.

"They look alike but each has a distinctive personality," Natalie was saying with those tantalizing lips.

He looked away, focusing on her girls. He'd come here to be a friend to Justin's widow, not to get her into bed.

"I can see that," he said. They were precocious, cute and as unique as they were alike.

"And to answer your question, yes, they occasionally switch roles and drive the rest of the world crazy, including me."

"Life can't be dull."

"Not for a moment." Natalie's dimples flashed. He'd always thought she had the cutest dimples and long ago had even entertained thoughts of exploring them with his tongue.

Great. There he went again. He really was losing his mind.

Before the twins had burst onto the scene,

he'd been tempted to kiss her. Now the insane urge was back. Natalie, with a pair of chopsticks holding her hair in a messy wad on top of her head and wearing a baker's coat over an old sweater and leggings, shouldn't have been the least bit attractive. But Cooper thought she was adorable. Add the bow mouth and peek-a-boo dimples and she was sexy in a way that defied explanation.

She licked those maddening lips, and his thoughts tumbled south. Way south. She was sexy, all right.

Whoa, Sullivan. Stop right there and get a grip. Remember why you're here. Natalie is your buddy's woman.

Widow, his evil imp whispered.

And he felt like a jerk. Even more so because he knew himself too well. He kissed. He made love. He did not — could not — become enmeshed in serious romantic relationships. His work required all of him. Someday he wanted a wife and family, but that day was in the future — far in the future, after he'd reached his goals. A man like him didn't go messing with his dead friend's wife.

Natalie blinked at him and he could swear she'd read his thoughts. Her dimples disappeared.

One of the twins, Lily, he thought, tugged on his hand and looked up with wide gray eyes.

"Are you a doctor like my daddy?"

Natalie answered for him. "He's a different kind of doctor. He fixes hearts."

"Oh. Can you fix my doll? Her leg fell off."

"Hearts, Lily, not legs," Rose said. "Don't you know the difference?"

Lily looked so crestfallen, Cooper couldn't disappoint the little girl. "Hearts or legs, makes no difference to me. I'll give it a shot. Bring your dolly in here."

"Oh, she doesn't need a shot. Just a little operation. I'll get her. She's asleep in her car." Lily skipped out of the kitchen. Rose made a mooching sound in the direction of her invisible dog and followed.

Natalie turned amused eyes his way. "Barbie lost a limb during a tug of war contest."

"Who won?"

"Not Barbie."

A moment later Lily returned without her sister, bearing her one-legged doll.

With all due seriousness, Cooper crouched down and took the toy, studying the dismembered limb with care.

Lily waited with a quiet expectancy that touched him. Justin should have been here to do these things for his child. Sometimes

67

life sucked.

"I'll need a good nurse to help me," he said.

"I'll help," Lily offered with an eagerness that pinched Cooper's heart. "I'm a good nurse, aren't I, Mom?"

"Absolutely." Natalie had returned to her cake icings and was busily stirring drops of color into each one. Cooper tried to focus on the doll instead of on Natalie's luscious little curves.

"All right, then, Nurse Lily. A detached limb presents a number of interesting problems. See this joint right here?" He pointed to the gaping hole in the bottom of the doll. "That's a ball-and-socket joint."

Lily, gray eyes wide, nodded. "Is that bad?"

"Well, the socket isn't bad. It just needs the ball to make it complete. You have the same joints in you." He held up the plastic leg. "And this upper section is called a femur. The ball of the femur fits neatly into this socket. Or it should."

"Oh." She put a hand on his shoulder and leaned forward, forehead wrinkled in concentration. Cooper felt a big splash right in the center of his chest.

"I think we might need some Super Glue, if your mom has any of that around."

"I use royal icing instead," Natalie chimed in. "Spread that on anything and it will stick for years."

"No Super Glue?"

"Sorry."

"Then royal icing, it is. Nurse Lily, would you please obtain some icing for our patient?"

"Yes, Doctor," Lily said with a giggle. She took the proffered container from Natalie, who stood, arms crossed, watching with a sweet smile on her face. Powdered sugar dusted one cheekbone.

Cooper had the strangest urge to do something impressive.

"If you will hold the patient," he told Lily. "I'll apply the medication." He gave her wink. "And then we'll lick the rest off our fingers."

The child grinned and took the doll, holding her exactly as Cooper indicated. He stuck his finger into the icing, applied it to the ball of the plastic femur, then shoved the limb into place with a loud pop.

"There," he said triumphantly. "All fixed. Barbie will run again. Thank you, Nurse Lily."

"You are the best doctor ever," Lily replied. "I bet you could help us find a really good Christmas tree, too." Following that out of context comment, she took the doll and bolted toward the door, shouting, "Rose. Cooper fixed my doll. With Mom's icing."

Cooper stood up and found Natalie watching him, eyes shining with amusement.

"That was a really nice thing to do, Cooper. And funny, too. Thank you. You made her day."

His sense of accomplishment was entirely out of proportion. "Cute kids."

"They're good girls. Mischievous sometimes, whirlwinds, but funny and loving and smart."

He could see that. He could also see how much the loss of their dad had affected them and how much they were missing because Justin wasn't here. His classmate would have been a good father. He would have wanted his girls to have everything, especially his attention.

It was a crying shame he'd left no insurance. If he remembered Justin, and he did, his buddy lived large. Unlike Cooper, Justin didn't come from money. He'd lived on loans and scholarships.

"So, what's the deal about a Christmas tree?" he asked.

Natalie waved off the question as she

70

fumbled with the beaters on a sad-looking mixer. "They were asking this morning. As soon as I have time we'll go to a lot and buy one."

"A real one?"

"Yes. It's become a tradition for the girls and me. Something they look forward to. Stomping around in the snow, freezing, drinking hot chocolate."

"The whole enchilada?"

Moving about the kitchen as they talked, she paused to grin. "Yes. I love traditions."

He hadn't known that about her. Back in the day, he'd been focused on other things. In fact, he didn't know a lot about the real Natalie, other than that she looked hot in a short skirt and her mouth fascinated him. But now he wanted to know her better. She deserved that. As Justin's widow, of course. He, on the other hand, would have to keep his less-than-brotherly thoughts to himself.

"Sappy movies, too?" he asked.

Blue eyes sparkled. "They're my best friends."

He emitted an appropriate male groan. "Chick flicks."

She giggled and made a face, all the while struggling with the mixer.

"What's wrong with your mixer?"

"I don't know. It's cantankerous at times."

Scooting her out of the way with his body, he took the machine in his hands for an examination. "Hmm."

She stuck close to his side, an attractive presence. He could feel the heat from her little body and smell the gentle scent of something floral amidst the baked goods. Distracting. Quite distracting. Not the least bit sisterly.

"What's the diagnosis, Doc? Can you save the patient?"

Though he had altered, invented and repaired any number of surgical tools, this was not a tool he understood. "I think you need a new one. This one smells over-heated."

"As long as it works, I'm happy." She took the mixer back in hand and jammed a strange looking apparatus into the connectors.

Stepping back, he let his gaze roam around the small duplex. Furnishings were neat and tidy but sparse. He frowned.

I've got your back, buddy. Cooper could almost hear the familiar phrase Justin tossed his way each time they scrubbed in together on a difficult case. Sure, they competed long and hard for rank, but if ever he needed help in the OR or on a test, Justin had been there. Funny how he'd let differences make him forget that bond.

What would Justin do if it had been Cooper who had left behind a wife and kids? With another glance at the worn-out mixer, he knew the answer, and just as certainly he knew what honor bade him do.

Emotion swelled inside his chest, tight and hot. "I've got your back, buddy," he silently whispered. "I've got your back."

If Natalie was struggling financially, he had a responsibility to Justin to help out. He'd always liked Natalie. He'd even tried to date her at one time, but that was before she'd gravitated toward Justin instead of him. When Justin had walked away with the prize, he'd not only been stunned, he'd awakened to the fact he was a jerk of the first order. He'd competed for a woman, not out of love, but to prove he could win. What kind of man did that make him?

A man that owed his friend a lot. The least he could do was make sure Justin's widow and children were well cared for.

I've got your back, buddy.

"Natalie?"

"Mmm-hmm?" She questioned, now spooning white icing into a funnel-shaped thing.

"How are you doing? I mean, really doing?"

She paused, a spatula at shoulder level. "We're okay."

She wasn't going to make this easy. "Justin left no insurance. Right?"

A wariness jumped into her blue, blue eyes. "I shouldn't have mentioned that."

"Yes, you should have. We're friends." When she lifted a pretty eyebrow, reminding him that friends didn't stay away for years, he said, "Time isn't an issue."

Actually, it was. The fact that he'd stayed away for so long and hadn't even known about Justin's death added to his burden of guilt.

Extending a frosting-loaded spatula, Natalie said, "Here. You get the spoon."

He looked at the plastic utensil in bewilderment. What did this have to do with their conversation? "It's purple."

"Food coloring has no flavor. Try it. I need your learned opinion."

With an exasperated sigh, he took a lick. "It's great. Look, I don't know how else to say this except straight out. I'd like to help you."

"Is the frosting that bad?"

"What?" He blinked at her and then at the spatula. "No. Come on, Natalie, stop dancing around the subject. I want to help you and the twins."

Wariness sprang into her expression. "Help us? In what way?"

He shifted, uncomfortable but determined. "Financially."

She yanked the spatula from his hand, her mouth forming a tight little smile. "I don't need financial help, Cooper. We're fine."

Turning her back, she retreated further into the kitchen to poke her head into a cabinet.

Cooper followed. "No, you're not."

She slammed the cabinet door with a resounding bang. The chopsticks in her hair quivered like antennae. "Excuse me?"

Blue eyes arced fire.

He'd started this and he'd be darned if he'd back down now. No peanut of a woman was going to scare him away from doing the right thing.

"It's pretty obvious that you're struggling to make ends meet. Justin was my friend. You're my friend. Money is not an issue with me. You know that." Fully aware he was sinking fast, he blew out a frustrated gust of air. "Throw me a bone here, Nat. I'm trying to be the good guy."

The tiny woman he'd once called "gnat" instead of Nat drew up to her full height.

"Let me be clear about something, Cooper. The girls and I are doing fine. We make

75

our own way. We depend on no one. I appreciate the sweet thought but do not trouble yourself about us."

Had she always been this exasperating? "It's not trouble! It's my responsibility. You need help. I can give it. Justin would expect it. And that's all there is to it."

"No, Cooper. That's not all there is to it. Now, please, can we drop this subject? You're nice to offer, but the answer is no."

"No?" She was telling him no?

Her gentle smile did nothing to ease the sharp stick of rejection. He was trying to do something good. Couldn't she get that? Justin would want this. He would expect his friends to come alongside Natalie and lend a hand. How could he keep an unspoken promise to a dead man without her cooperation?

As if the conversation was closed — which it was not, at least as far as he was concerned — Natalie picked up the white funnellike bag and began squeezing pretty purple flowers onto the edge of a sheet cake.

What was wrong with this woman? Ninety percent of the women he knew found his bank account extremely attractive. So much so that he was generally wary. So, why did Natalie behave as if he'd propositioned her for sex on the subway? The Natalie he'd once known wasn't prickly. Was she so into the liberated female mode that she couldn't appreciate fresh, green money?

A bad feeling crept over him.

Maybe it wasn't money she didn't appreciate.

Maybe it was him.

Natalie wasn't sure if she was more upset because Cooper had offered money or because she'd thought he'd come to offer something else — like a date.

She was completely losing her mind. That's what it was. That's why she'd thought he'd been looking at her mouth and thinking about kissing her, when he'd only been searching for a way to provide financial assistance.

Sheesh. "Stupid" was her middle name.

The offer was kind. Really it was. That was the trouble. Pity, like alum, left a bad taste in the mouth.

Long after he'd left, she slammed pans and piped pansies until she was exhausted. The twins roamed in and out of the kitchen, accustomed to their Mom's obsession with baking. Anytime she was upset, she baked. And baked. And baked. Thank goodness her emotional turmoil produced something profitable.

Finally, when the last cake rested on the cooling rack and her shoulders ached, she fixed the girls a bowl of chowder and then headed to her bedroom for five minutes of peace and quiet and a hot shower.

Justin's face smiled out at her from a picture frame on the dresser. She wanted to slap the smile right off his handsome face. Some days she was still so mad at him, and today was one of those days. How dare he leave her in a position to be embarrassed by Cooper Sullivan's pity?

She picked up the gilt-edged frame and stared down into laughing gray eyes. A sudden dose of heavy heart pressed her down onto the side of the bed.

She knew the stages of grief, had read the coping books given to her by concerned friends, and most of the time she handled the loss well. Over the last two years, the various emotions had come and gone, ebbing and flowing until she'd accepted the inevitable. Justin was not coming back and she had to move on with her life. She *was* moving on with her life. Then, some little thing, a sound, a smell, a memory, would trigger the anger. It was so much easier to be mad at him than to think of all he would miss, of all she and the girls would miss because he was gone.

"How could anyone so smart be so stupid?" she said, resisting the tears that burned her nose.

She could almost hear him say, "Stop worrying, babe. You know I'll take care of you."

But he hadn't.

Neither would Cooper Sullivan, or any other man, for that matter. She would never again risk the terror of having her entire life jerked out from under her. The stunning reality that she was on her own, the only parent to two kids, the provider, the *everything,* when she hadn't known how to be any of those things, had been more than she'd ever wanted to face again. In two years she'd learned a lot.

She would never go back to helplessly depending on a doting man.

"Mom, is Dr. Cooper gone?"

The small voice came from behind her. Madly she batted her eyes to dry the tears. Her girls fretted enough without seeing their mommy cry over nothing.

"Yes, sweetie," she said, turning with a fake smile.

"I like him. He fixed my doll. He's nice." Lily's pretty face carried a gentle, wistful expression. Natalie hurt to know how much Lily missed the relationship she'd had with her father.

"Mmm. Nice? Yes, I guess so." Cooper had always been charming, but today he'd embarrassed her. He'd also made her mad.

"Rose said he wanted to be your boyfriend."

Justin's picture clutched to her chest like a shield, she gaped at her daughter. "What?"

"It's okay if you like him, Mom. I do, too. He can be your boyfriend. We need a daddy around here sometimes."

"Oh, Lily." One of the tears she'd been holding back slipped out. "We don't need a daddy."

As she said the words, Natalie recognized the lie. Her girls *did* need a daddy. The problem was, she didn't need a man.

Particularly not Cooper Sullivan.

CHAPTER FOUR

A sharp wind whipped Cooper's coat out behind him as he bounded up the steps of the Wedding Belles' Building, package in hand. He liked old historical buildings, and if he hadn't been in a hurry to get back to his office, he would have paused to enjoy the restored facility. He'd left a mountain of work, had three consults and a surgery less than an hour from now. He glanced at his watch. In and out, accomplish the mission and try not to enjoy it too much.

He still couldn't get over the way Natalie had responded to a simple solution to an obvious problem. The aggravating, stubborn woman had turned him down. Turned him down and shown him the door. He couldn't believe it. He, Cooper Sullivan, had been shot down during a random act of kindness. In trying to help, he'd embarrassed and angered her. He must be losing his touch. Either that, or being in Natalie's kitchen surrounded by her cakes and kids and her curvy little body, he'd been too rattled and out of his element to handle things correctly.

He still wasn't sure why he'd gone to her house at all, but once there he'd understood the mission. He was going to help her whether she liked it or not. For Justin's sake. In Justin's memory. It was the least he could do. He wouldn't rest until she surrendered to his will. To do less would be wrong, and he was already having enough trouble with his conscience where she was concerned. He didn't need anything else to feel guilty about.

The door sucked closed behind him, and he entered what appeared to be an entirely feminine establishment. Pity the poor groom who was forced to enter. Cooper shivered. The place even smelled like matrimony.

Classy enough for the best of Boston, the Wedding Belles' reception area was taste and elegance in shades of gold and cream with reminders that the Christmas wedding season was in full swing. Tiny lights twinkled from a tree that Martha Stewart could have created. Above the fireplace mantel hung a fancy wreath and garland. Though the room fragrance was aptly cinnamon and pine, a perfectly appointed bouquet of white roses graced the front desk. Beautiful place, if a person wanted to get married. Even his mother would approve.

His collar had suddenly grown too snug. He tugged at it. No man wanted to be stuck in a wedding establishment for any length of time.

"May I help you, sir?" A distracted-looking redhead with a charming Aussie accent spoke from the reception desk. Her bright hair had been slicked back into some kind of controlled hairdo, but stubborn curls corkscrewed from the holder to bounce around her freckled face.

"I was wondering if Natalie is here. She didn't answer her phone."

Green eyes narrowed. "Are you a friend of hers?"

"A very old friend." He held up the shopping bag. "This is for her." Please take it and let me get out of here.

The redhead grinned. "You don't look old to me. Have a seat and I'll send Natalie this direction. She and the other Belles are back here doing taste tests."

Cooper settled onto one of the plush couches to wait. A grin pulled at the corners of his mouth. Did Natalie taste test everyone she encountered?

Almost before he'd finished that thought,

six female faces appeared around the adjacent doorway to peer at him. When he glanced up, they disappeared, but he could still hear their whispers. A moment later a pretty brunette with a camera slung around her neck emerged alone.

"Julie said Natalie had a caller. You must be Cooper."

He stood. "Have we met?"

"I'm Regina O'Ryan, Natalie's friend. I saw the two of you at the Craggin wedding. She told me about you."

She did?

"Ah. Nice wedding. You're the photographer?" He motioned to the skillfully grouped black-and-white photos hanging on the walls. "These are good."

"Yes, those are my babies." Pride shone on her classically pretty face but she didn't elaborate on her professional expertise. "You and Natalie looked really cute dancing together. She told me you saved her from an insulin reaction."

"It took me a minute to realize what was happening. I'd forgotten she was a diabetic."

"So you're a doctor?"

"Pediatric heart surgeon. Natalie's husband and I attended med school together."

"Cool. What's your interest in my friend?"

He laughed. He liked this gal.

"Nothing kinky." He was determined to keep that in mind.

"Too bad." She covered a laugh and glanced around to see if she'd been heard. "Forget I said that."

"I take it the two of you are good friends."

"The best. Nat's a jewel."

"I suppose she has her struggles, raising two girls alone."

Regina gave him a coolly appraising once over. "She's strong and smart. She can handle it."

It? Meaning, of course, that there was something to handle. What was it? Debts? Day-to-day essentials? A new car?

Before he could press for more information, a gaggle of women gushed through the front door.

The photographer, whose hands never strayed far from her camera reacted. "Oh, sorry. It was great meeting you, Cooper, but I have a photo meeting with a bridal party. Natalie should be along any minute now."

She greeted the women and ushered them out of the room, leaving him convinced. Natalie needed him more than he'd thought.

Natalie's heart slammed against her rib cage with the force of a metro bus as she stopped dead still in the arched entryway. Looking sexy and confident in a maroon pullover sweater atop a blue dress shirt, Cooper stood in the reception area. Just what she did *not* need.

"Cooper! What in the world are you doing here?" she blurted.

Belle, voice dripping with Southern charm didn't give him a chance to answer. "Now, Natalie, honey, that is no way to greet a gentleman caller."

Gentleman caller. Good grief. Leave it to Belle to see romance where there was none. Absolutely none, given that Cooper didn't see her as woman. He saw her as a pitiful creature who needed his assistance. Apparently, she hadn't made herself clear. Not that she wanted to hurt his feelings, but with the palpitations he caused, she'd be better off not seeing him at all.

"Sorry, Cooper. I'm just surprised to see you."

"Oh, so this is *Cooper?*" Serena James, the Belles' dress designer gave him the once-over. With her blond beauty she could have had him eating out of her palm in five minutes, but as Natalie well knew, Serena had already met her match in Kane Wiley. Funny how glad Natalie was about that.

"Cooper Sullivan, meet my friends and

coworkers, Serena and Callie. You've met Julie our fabulous girl Friday. And of course, Belle, our boss and surrogate mom."

Following the introductions, Natalie expected her friends to disappear. She should have known better. With unabashed speculation, all of them loitered in the reception area, eyes sparkling in a way that made Natalie want to scream. She was not interested in Cooper. Could not ever be interested in someone like him. He was far too much like Justin with his freewheeling, big-spending, cocky attitude.

The truth was, Natalie didn't quite know what to do with him. Unless he'd changed a lot, he was a good guy as far as playboy types could be labeled good. And she hated to hurt anyone's feelings, but what was he doing here?

She was about to ask when Belle drawled in her best Southern accent, "Cooper, honey, would you care to come back to the kitchenette for some of Natalie's cake. She is the finest baker in the entire city of Boston. Why, her Hummingbird Cake reminds me of my mama's banana puddin'."

Natalie rolled her eyes at Belle's obvious machinations. "Cooper has to get back to the hospital. Don't you, Cooper?"

He glanced at his watch and nodded

before turning a dazzling smile toward Belle. "May I take a rain check on that invitation?"

"Anytime at all, honey." Belle patted his arm. "Please give my compliments to your mama. Your manners are lovely."

Oh, boy, just what she didn't need. Belle going ga-ga over him and his impeccable manners. She was already having enough problems with Lily. Her daughter had developed an instant fixation on the man who'd repaired her doll with royal icing.

"Belle, don't you and Charlie have a date or something?"

While the other ladies tittered, Belle flushed, and for one of those rare moments had nothing to say.

Serena, who had been fiddling with a display mannequin's wedding train while she listened in on every word, spoke up instead. "Natalie, we'll all finished up here. Why don't you have Cooper drive you home?"

Natalie ground her teeth. Serena knew very well she drove a rattling old van to transport her cakes. "Because I have my vehicle?"

And also because she was not going to be Dr. Sullivan's charity case.

"Well, leave it here. You can always catch

the T in tomorrow morning." Callie grinned, green eyes starry. Just back from a fabulous honeymoon with her new husband, she hadn't made any sense all week and this time was no exception.

"It isn't every day a handsome doctor offers to drive you home," beautiful Serena put in.

Heat rushed up Natalie's neck. Why did Cooper have to come to the business where her misguided friends could meet him and start in on her? Just because all the Belles except Audra and her had found their soul mates did not mean Natalie wanted to follow in their footsteps. She'd fought long and hard to stand on her own two feet. She would not relinquish control to anyone.

"He didn't offer, Serena, in case you missed that part of our conversation." Which seemed impossible, given how big her ears had grown in the last three minutes. "He's on his way back to the hospital which happens to be *that* direction." She pointed northeast, the opposite way of her duplex.

Cooper took pity on her. Again. "I do have to run. I just stopped by to give you this." He thrust a Macy's shopping bag into her hands. Her arm buckled with the weight.

She looked at it, bewildered. What ever could it be? "No, Cooper."

She tried to hand it back.

His charming smile evaporated. He held up a hand. "Subject is closed. No refunds, and I sure don't need the thing."

She was floundering fast. How did one refuse a gift without being rude and ungrateful?

She didn't.

"Thank you," she said meekly.

"Aren't you going to open it?"

The other Belles crowded in, now joined by their bookkeeper, Audra, who seldom left her structured domain. Cooper had drawn a crowd. Poor Regina was the only person in the place who was actually working.

Natalie fought the urge to laugh hysterically as she reached into the shopping bag and lifted out a huge box. "Oh my goodness. I've always wanted one of these."

Audra whistled softly. "Top of the line. The man knows his mixers."

Leave it to the bean counter to know the value of a kitchen mixer.

"Cooper, I can't accept this."

"Of course you can," Audra said. "You need it. Last week when we played cards at your house, we waited thirty minutes for your old beat-up mixer to cool down before you could frost our tarts."

"We nearly swooned from the wait," Serena added, a wicked gleam in her eyes. "Cooper, you have saved all of us with your amazing taste. We are ever in your debt."

Chuckling and clucking like happy hens, the group murmured approval of Cooper's gift. The truth was, she loved it, too. Having a mixer of this quality with all the bells and whistles would speed things up considerably.

No one mentioned the obvious — that a mixer was a strange gift, the kind of thing you gave to your grandmother. If anything, this should prove to the Belles as it did to her that Cooper was not interested in her as a woman, only as Justin's poor, pathetic widow. She should be glad about that. And she was. Really, she was.

"I love it. Thank you," she said, if a little stiffly.

Cooper didn't seem to notice. The thrill of victory radiated from him. "So, are we going after that tree later or what?"

She blinked at him, totally dumbfounded. "Tree?"

"As in Christmas. Freezing snow, hot chocolate, the whole enchilada?" he said, eyes twinkling as he repeated their conversation from last Saturday. "I know the perfect place."

The offer was way too appealing. She shook her head no. Hadn't he done enough for one day? "Can't. Too much work to do."

"Nonsense," Belle said. "Except for my meeting at four with the Dorcetts, we're all caught up here."

She turned exasperated eyes to her boss. "Belle."

The buxom Belle laughed her rich throaty laugh. "Okay, girls, come on. Clear out and let Natalie have a minute with her beau."

"He's not my —" Oh, what was the use? She flopped down onto a fussy little brocade chair and waited for the other women to evacuate the room. All except Julie, who had been so distracted lately planning her own wedding, she didn't notice much of anything, anyway.

Cooper stood in front of her, hands on hips, his eyes dancing with laughter. "I like them."

"Me, too. But I apologize for their outrageous behavior."

"They care about you."

A warmth spread through her. "Yes."

If it hadn't been for the Belles, she didn't know what she would have done during the past two years. They had been friends, family, shoulders to cry on, and even if they did stick their noses into each other's business,

92

it was out of love.

"So, how about if we make them happy and go get that tree?"

"Cooper, I told you. I don't need your charity."

"I could let you pay for the hot chocolate."

In spite of herself, she laughed. "You wouldn't."

"No, but it was worth a try."

And there was the crux of the matter. Cooper, like Justin, wanted to take control. But unlike Justin, he didn't love her. Thank goodness. She didn't need that kind of stress in her life. But she did need that Christmas tree.

"If you won't let me do anything for *you*, let me do it for the twins," he said. "I wasn't here two years ago, Natalie. That bothers me. Let me do this for Justin's little girls."

"You don't play fair."

His smile was unapologetic acknowledgment. "Six o'clock?"

The girls would be ecstatic. And putting up a live Christmas tree with only children to help was not an easy task.

She was going to give in. Just this once. She hoped she wouldn't regret it.

Cooper was pretty sure he was losing his mind, but, for the first time since he'd returned to Boston, he felt as though he'd accomplished something worthwhile. How stupid was that? He'd gotten Natalie to agree to go out for a Christmas tree. Big achievement. And yet, he knew this was the right thing to do.

Adorably stubborn woman. From this point on, he would do a lot more things to help her. All in Justin's memory, of course. Eventually she would come around to his way of thinking.

As he wove his SUV through the residential section to her duplex, he thought of the work he should be doing tonight. He was presenting a paper to a conference in New York in two weeks and again in Zurich come January. The work was done, but there was always more to research, more to learn, more to improve. His mind itched with the exciting possibilities his profession presented.

But he could work later after the tree was purchased and decorated. Late nights never killed him.

The thought stopped him cold. Late nights had killed Justin. Late nights and the desire to have it all — career, family, adventure.

As he pulled up to the curb outside the older, dark-green duplex, two little girls in

94

bright-red coats and boots tumbled down the wooden steps. He couldn't stop the smile that spread through him as he heard their excited squeals above his CD player. Behind them, in a heavy coat, pale hair peeking from beneath a knitted hat, came Natalie, her face much more serious than the girls'. For once there were no projectiles poking up from her head. Before he could get out to open the doors, all three had piled into his vehicle, bringing with them the smell of winter and Natalie's sugar-and-spice fragrance.

One look at her and he had to remind himself that he was here for Justin on a temporary basis. See to Natalie's needs and then move on, as he always did. No time to indulge in dimples and smiles and sweetly baked cakes.

"Mom says you're taking us to get our Christmas tree," one twin said from the back seat on the right, angelic face framed in a tightly secured hood.

The other twin leaned forward from behind him. "Can we get a big one? My friend Ashley's touches the ceiling."

"Lily. Don't," Rose cautioned. "Mom said we had to be polite and not ask for stuff. Are we being polite, Cooper?"

"So far, so good," he answered. His car

had gone from quiet and empty to completely alive. The weird thing was he liked it.

By now Natalie was beside him on the front seat securing her seat belt. "Buckle up, girls."

Obediently they both sat back and complied.

Natalie smiled over at him, a smile that didn't quite reach those baby blues. "I don't know how I let you talk me into this."

"What? You don't want a Christmas tree?"

"You already know the answer to that."

In other words, it was him that wasn't wanted. Cool. Good, actually. No strings, no entanglements. "If I'm pushing in on something reserved for family just say so."

"Don't be silly."

But he wondered. And that made him all the more determined to show her a good time.

He put the car into gear and headed down the street. Dirty snow piled along the sides where the plows had made their run. Here and there a snowman waved, and Christmas lights blinked red and green from the eaves of houses.

"I like your car," a little voice said from behind him. He glanced in the mirror at Rose. He'd figured out which was which by listening to their chatter. "Mama's van is all rattley and bumpy."

Natalie shot her daughter an exasperated look. "That's because it's a cargo van. They all rattle."

"I still like Cooper's better."

Cooper pressed a button and activated the DVD player in the back seat. "Maybe you'll like this even more. How about a movie?"

"Cool. Mom, look, there's a DVD player back here."

"With movies and everything," Lily said in awe.

Instead of the pleasure he'd expected to see on Natalie's face, she frowned.

"Don't you let your girls watch movies?"

"Yes, of course."

"Then what's wrong?"

"Nothing." She stared out at the rapidly falling darkness and grew quiet. Whatever he'd done, she wasn't going to tell him.

He tried anyway. "Penny for your thoughts."

"I'm thinking you just drove past a lot full of trees."

"I have a tree farm in mind. It's further out of the city, but I think the girls will like it."

"Now I'm curious. Where are we going?"

"You'll see."

She didn't press. "How did the surgery go?"

He jacked a questioning eyebrow.

Natalie answered, "Weren't you headed off to surgery after embarrassing me at the Wedding Belles?"

He laughed. "I didn't mean to embarrass you."

"But you like getting your way."

"Doesn't everyone?"

"I suppose."

"To answer your question, the surgery went fairly well, all things considered. A newborn with transposition of the great arteries. We repaired those and a ventricle defect, but she's not out of the woods."

She listened with earnest attention, one of those rare people outside medicine that didn't ask for definitions. No doubt she'd become familiar with such terms by giving Justin this same rapt attention.

"How are her parents doing?"

He glanced at her, impressed with the question. In the golden glow of dash lights, her face was in soft shadow. He couldn't quite read her, but he could feel her. The knowledge unsettled him.

"Standing strong. They have great faith that she'll make it."

"And a great doctor."

With a grin he shrugged. "There is that. Neonatal surgery is my area of expertise."

She gave his arm a playful swat. "Conceit."

He rubbed the spot. "There's a difference between conceit and confidence. If I don't believe I can do the job, my patients are in trouble."

One thing he'd never lacked was confidence in the OR. It was as if something magical happened to him when he scrubbed in. The rest of the world disappeared and the present case became his universe. He never wanted to walk out of an operating room and wonder if he could have done more. He gave it everything he had, every time. Even if he had to study a case for weeks, he made darn sure he had the knowledge and the tools before going in. He was good because he had to be.

He was honest, too. He worked harder, studied more, researched for hours on end, because the ultimate goal grew closer with every surgery. If he relaxed now, someone else would step in to take his place.

By now, they'd left the city and were nearing the tree farm. The quieter countryside rolled by. Lights from farm houses dotted the darkness like stars in an inky sky.

He couldn't wait for the twins to see his surprise.

"How's the movie, girls?"

"It's got Santa in it!"

Cooper glanced at Natalie. She was smiling.

"Can we watch another one?" asked Lily.

"Look outside the window first. See those lights?" He tapped his side glass.

"Christmas lights! Is this the place?"

"That's it." He turned down the lane lined with twinkling lights where soaring pines and furs practically touched the clouds. Up ahead was his surprise.

"What is that?" Natalie asked, straining forward to squint into the shadows ahead.

Cooper didn't answer. Instead he pulled into a small, graveled parking area and hopped out of the vehicle. The cold air, while sharp, wasn't unbearable. An occasional snowflake swirled to the ground. It was a perfect December night for Christmas tree shopping.

Doors slammed as his guests jumped out and joined him. Natalie's breath puffed white as she spoke. Excitement, reminiscent of the girl he remembered from college, emanated from her. "Oh, Cooper, that is so perfect. The twins will love it."

Her pleasure pleased him more than it should. For Justin, he reminded himself. He was only here to do what Justin couldn't.

A miniature train painted with elves and Santa faces waited to take them through the rows and rows of towering trees and then into the warming barn where other goodies awaited them.

"Can we ride? Can we, Mom?"

"That's what we came for," Cooper said. While the words still hung in the night air, the twins were off, running toward the open cars. They scrambled aboard, chattering and giggling in a way that would make anyone happy. This was what Christmas was all about. Kids, family.

Some of his pleasure seeped away, though he wasn't sure why. The feeling that he was missing something persisted.

"Come on, Mom," one of the kids called. "It's fun."

Cooper grabbed Natalie's hand and jogged with her to the train.

A farmer in bright-red overalls and a striped engineer's cap greeted them. "You folks looking for a tree?"

"A big one," Rose said. "Big as the sky."

"I know just the one." He chucked Rose under the chin. "You little ladies like sugar cookies?"

"Sure. Our mom is a cake fairy. She makes good cookies."

"Is that a fact?"

"Yes." The twins and the farmer kept up a running conversation as the train chugged to life and started to wind along the narrow track.

Natalie and Cooper settled in the seat directly behind Lily and Rose. The cars were small, squeezing them tightly against one another. And if Cooper enjoyed the press of Natalie's curvy body against his more than he ought to have, there was really nothing he could do about it.

"This is fun, Cooper," Natalie said, her breath puffing out in warm clouds as the train chugged slowly into the rows of towering pine and fir. "The girls are loving it."

"What about their mom?" Funny how important that was to him. The girls were impressed. He wanted Natalie to be as well. "Does she love it, too?"

"It's great. Truly. I really appreciate it."

Her lips curved into a beautiful smile that caused his belly to flip-flop. Before he could stop his thoughts, they had gone off in the wrong direction again. She had the most kissable mouth in Massachusetts. Maybe in the world. Just one kiss. That's all he wanted. To see if she tasted as sweet as her cake icing.

With the self-control that had made him a super surgeon, Cooper forced his gaze away from her mouth. But staring off into the dark shadowy tree field didn't erase the images in his head. The woman touched him from shoulder to ankle. She smelled like sugar cookies and summertime. He could see those tiny puffs of white breath as she laughed and exclaimed over the whimsical decorations hidden here and there in the tree grove. She was real; she was alive; she was maddening.

She was Justin's widow.

How was a man supposed to concentrate?

Deep inside the huge field, the train sputtered to a stop.

Cooper faced the inevitable disembarking with both relief and regret. But when everyone scattered up and down the rows to find the perfect tree, he didn't resist taking Natalie's hand again as they strolled. No big deal. Just friends finding a Christmas tree.

Then why did he notice the way her eyes sparkled brighter beneath the lights? And why did his stomach dip every time she laughed that magical, tinkling laugh? The wild urge to kiss her was back.

"Cooper?" Natalie's voice was hushed.

He gazed down at her, standing small and snow kissed at his side. "Yeah?"

"You have a funny look on your face. Is

something wrong?"

He smiled and stepped closer. Yes, something was wrong. He would die if he didn't kiss her.

Natalie tilted her head, eyes questioning. A tiny pulse beat at the base of her throat. From somewhere up ahead, the twins' voices carried on the wind.

He tugged on Natalie's hand, drawing her closer. *Give me a sign, any sign that she won't slap my face.*

The tiny pulse picked up pace.

"Cooper?" she said again but didn't resist. When their bodies were aligned, he slid both arms around her and waited for her reaction. For a second she stiffened but just as quickly relaxed. She wasn't fighting him. Maybe she was even inviting him.

Oh, man. He was dying.

The night air was cold and still and pungent with evergreen. The pulse in her throat had somehow moved into his chest.

He was losing his mind, but he had to kiss her.

"Let's celebrate," he said quietly.

"Celebrate what?" Her words came a little short, a little breathy.

"Renewed friendship," he murmured. And before his conscience could start up again, he bowed his head and tasted heaven.

CHAPTER FIVE

"Mommy!"

At the sound of her daughter's voice, Natalie sprang away from Cooper and stumbled backward into a prickly pine. Unbalanced by the sudden move, Cooper tottered on the verge of tumbling down on top of her. At the last possible second, he caught her outstretched hand and yanked her upright.

Flushed and flustered, Natalie dusted pine needles from her clothes and avoided Cooper's eyes. Her mouth still tingled from the brief whisper of a kiss that had, shamefully, left her wishing for more.

She had the most embarrassing desire to touch her lips.

"Are you okay?" Cooper's voice was strained as his doctor's hands gripped her shoulders.

"Fine."

"Mommy?"

She glanced up to find Rose standing at

the end of the row. Worry puckered her brow.

"What is it, honey?" Natalie asked, not at all surprised to find her breath annoyingly short.

"What are you doing?"

I was kissing a man that I shouldn't have, she was tempted to reply, though Rose had likely already figured that part out. Worse, she'd probably witnessed it.

"Looking at this tree," she answered. "Come see."

Was she a terrible person for lying to her child? She didn't know. At the moment, she was rattled. What had Cooper been thinking to do such a thing? Worse yet were her own disturbing thoughts. His gentle touch, his soft kiss had stirred something long buried. Something scary that she would as soon leave alone.

It had been such a long time since she'd been kissed. Or even held for that matter. Surely that was why such a little kiss had seemed powerful enough to bring her to her knees. If Rose hadn't intervened, Natalie had no doubt she would have pressed closer and kissed him back.

Thank goodness for her nosy child. She had no desire to be a notch on Cooper's trophy shelf.

Rose didn't move. She stood five feet away, her expression contemplative. "I want to go home."

"But, honey, we came to choose our tree. Come on now. What do you think of this one? It's a little tall but shaped very nicely."

"Okay." Rose lacked her usual enthusiasm.

"Go get Lily and we'll ask her opinion, too."

Rose's gaze flashed to Cooper. "I don't want to."

Rose had either witnessed the kiss or suspected it. Either way, she was not a happy camper. Earlier, Cooper had risen to superhero status, but now Rose shot him a dagger stare.

"Why don't we all go find her? This tree isn't going anywhere," Cooper said, as smooth as warm honey and seemingly unaffected by their too-brief kiss. She, on the other hand, still battled raging hormones and a sense that she'd done something wrong. But she hadn't. She was a widow, not a wife. A woman with feelings and needs.

The problem was she'd neglected those needs for a very long time.

Rose relented. "Lily! Come out."

A giggle broke from somewhere behind them. Great. So Lily too had been lurking nearby during her mother's moment of weakness.

"Mama," Lily said as she reappeared from behind a giant Douglas fir. "Are you going to marry Cooper?"

Rose turned on her like a provoked badger. "Shut up, Lily, You shut up."

"Rose Isabella!" Natalie abhorred those words and never allowed her girls to say them. Dropping to her haunches, she caught Rose by the upper arms. "What is wrong with you?"

"I don't want you to get married."

Cooper crouched beside them and put on his best doctor's voice. "Rose, your mom and I are friends. We're both too busy with our careers to even think about getting married."

Cooper's words were like water on a fire. His career was his life and she was a busy mother, providing for her kids. Right. Good. That's the way it should be.

But Rose couldn't be expected to understand these things. Confusion flickered over her upturned face. Natalie's heart hurt. Clearly, Rose thought she was betraying Justin's memory.

"Really?" Rose asked. "You're not getting married?"

"Absolutely not." He almost shivered with

certainty. Natalie wasn't surprised at his adamancy, but it did sting a little. What was she? Chopped liver?

Good grief, she was as confused as Rose.

"Pinky promise?" The eight-year-old thrust a tiny finger toward Cooper, all crooked and ready.

Cooper grinned. "You drive a hard bargain. Are you planning to be a lawyer?"

He extended his pinky.

Rose grinned back. "Maybe. Or a doctor like my dad. He helped people get well."

No need to point out that Cooper did the same. Rose knew. She was doing battle for her daddy's memory, to keep him from being replaced.

It was a good thing Natalie never intended to remarry.

By now Lily, who seemed oblivious, was raring to go. "Come on, people. Mr. Fred and I found the most awesome, perfectest tree ever. Mr. Fred said it would make Ashley's look like a tomato plant."

They all chuckled, and the tense moment passed. But as the group trucked in the direction of Mr. Fred, Cooper didn't try to hold her hand again.

She was both relieved and disappointed.

"It's enormous."

Lily's perfect Christmas tree took up every extra inch of space in Natalie's tiny living room and permeated the duplex with its rich pine fragrance. She'd been reluctant to purchase one of such size, but the twins, with Cooper's help, had outnumbered her.

"Enormously beautiful," Cooper answered, looking proud as he adjusted the stand one last time. He flashed a killer smile in her direction. He'd been like this all evening. Charming, fun, kind to her girls. A little bit sexy.

Okay, a lot sexy.

Every time she looked at him, her neck grew warm and her heart bumped like some teenager with a crush.

To annihilate such thoughts, she flipped on some Christmas music and then dug into the cardboard box of decorations. She doubted they had anywhere near enough for their monstrous tree, but she wasn't about to put a damper on the twins' excitement. Decorations they could always create. The tree may not be designer perfect like the one at the office, but it would be covered with love.

"If you girls will help Cooper get started, I'll make popcorn."

"And hot chocolate?" Rose asked. "And sugar cookies?"

"You had cookies earlier tonight."

Her daughter looked disappointed. Rose's sweet tooth grew worse with age. "I bet Cooper would like more cookies. Wouldn't you, Cooper?"

He laughed. "Whatever your mother says."

Rose gave him a look of complete disgust but relented when he handed her one end of a string of lights. He had yet to win Rose's adoration. Lily, on the other hand, hung on every word and giggled appropriately.

Leaving her daughters and Cooper with the tree, Natalie maneuvered around the boxes into the kitchen. While waiting for the popcorn to pop, she listened to childish giggles and the warm baritone of Cooper's laugh as they teased and played and argued about the best way to drape lights. Between teasing disagreements, they took turns belting out snatches of silly Christmas carols. And after every one, the girls erupted in a fit of giggles.

Justin had never been here to decorate the tree. Not once. She and the girls had done it together while he'd been at work. It had always been a special occasion, but not festive like this.

Now, as she observed Lily and Rose basking in Cooper's attention, a hitch in her heart, she saw how much they'd missed. Part of her wanted to be mad at Cooper for coming along and reminding her of all that they'd lost. Part of her was grateful he was here, making this memory for her children.

Maybe Cooper had been a better friend than she'd given him credit for.

But he shouldn't have kissed her.

She dumped the buttery popcorn into a big wooden bowl and headed back into the living room. From the stereo, someone sang, "Let it snow, let it snow, let it snow." Natalie couldn't help thinking the singer must not live in New England.

"Here you go, guys. A dollar a handful."

"Cheap at twice the price." Cooper took a handful as Lily wound a long strand of tinsel around his neck, giggling all the while.

"Lily, let the poor man come up for air."

"He likes it, don't you Cooper?" Big gray eyes looked up at him with adoration.

"Every man needs a shiny silver scarf." He tossed the end of the tinsel dramatically over one shoulder.

"Mama," she said, "did you know Cooper sang in the choir when he was a little boy?"

"I didn't know that." She popped several kernels of corn into her mouth.

"And he broke his arm when he was seven. I never broke anything before."

"Boys are rowdier," he said.

For the first time, Natalie thought of Cooper as a little boy. He would have been adorable, all big, dark eyes and orneriness. He'd make beautiful children someday.

To stop that train of thought, she thrust the bowl of popcorn toward her daughter. "Rose, you want some popcorn?"

Rose had been unusually quiet while hooking brightly colored balls onto the limbs.

"No, but Puppy does." She cast a sly glance between Cooper and Lily.

"Don't start with that. Leave Puppy under the bed." Puppy had a bad habit of appearing whenever Rose wanted to misbehave.

"But he likes popcorn."

"Rose," she warned, giving her child a mother's version of the evil eye.

Small shoulders slumped in annoyance. "Okay. But he'll be really mad to miss out."

Lily laid aside a shiny Christmas ball. "I'll take him a bite." She dipped a handful of popcorn and headed out of the room.

"Did you ever consider getting them a real pet?" Cooper asked.

"No pets allowed."

"Not even a fish?"

"How much interaction does a child get from a fish?"

"About the same as from an invisible dog?" he said.

She made a face. "Good answer, Doc."

"Do you have a fish, Cooper?" Rose asked.

"A lot of them. I have an aquarium in my office."

"Can we see it sometime?" By now Lily had returned to putting baubles on the tree and paused to stare up at him with wide eyes.

"Anytime, princess." He glanced at Natalie. "Why not come by on Monday. I'll take you to lunch."

"We have school." From her expression Lily considered this the worst thing in her life. "Christmas break is not until the next week."

"Too bad. The offer is open anytime you can make it." He stood up from among the scattered tinsel, eyes never leaving Natalie's. Her heart took a funny lurch. "What about you, Natalie? Why not drop by on Monday and let me show you my office?"

"Is that where you keep your etchings?" She didn't know why she'd say such a foolish, suggestive thing, especially in front of the twins.

Cooper pumped one eyebrow. "No. Those are kept under lock and key in my condo." He offered an ornery wink. "Open invitation to see those anytime, too."

Natalie didn't know what had come over her, but she felt saucy and full of energy. "Are you trying to be a bad man in front of my girls?"

Rose piped up, "Puppy will bite him if he's bad."

Her comment broke the spell, and both adults burst into laughter. But Natalie liked the tingly, sexy zing in her blood. Even joking, Cooper made her remember what it felt like to be a woman. There was nothing wrong with remembering as long as she also kept in mind the most important and painful lesson she'd learned after Justin's death. Learning to survive on her own had come at a high price.

She dug out the last string of tired-looking garlands. "We're out of decorations, folks. This is the last hurrah. Such as it is."

Lily eyed it doubtfully. "Mom, half the shiny stuff is gone. It's naked."

"Think we should toss it?" she asked.

Three heads nodded.

She tossed the sad piece of garland high into the air. "Time to put on the star and call it a Christmas tree."

Both children clamored to add the topper. In the end, Cooper hoisted one in each arm and let them share the honor. At the sight,

Natalie's chest ached with some sweet, unnamed emotion.

"Ready to try the lights?" she asked, reaching for the wall switch to turn off the overhead bulb.

"Drum roll, please," Cooper said, green plug held dramatically aloft.

Lily and Rose each pretended to drum.

"Ta-da," Natalie announced as the tree lights blinked white and the sound of "Away in a Manger" tinkled from a strand of musical bells.

"It doesn't have much stuff." Standing between the tall man and the giant tree, Rose, lit by the flicker of Christmas colors, looked tiny and angelic. Natalie's heart squeezed. Most of the time Rose *was* an angel, but lately she'd been moody and cranky and sometimes naughty. Was there such a thing as the terrible eights?

"We can add some ornament cookies," Natalie suggested. "And paper angels with glitter."

"Tonight?" Rose asked hopefully.

"Maybe tomorrow. Tonight it's bedtime."

"No. Mom. No." Both girls protested as if they were being sent to the firing squad.

"Sorry, my sweeties. Head for the bath."

"But, Mom!"

"Sorry. Go on now. I'll come and tuck you

116

in when you're ready."

"Can we have a story?" Rose asked, always working an angle to stall for time.

"A Christmas story?" Lily put in.

"Sure." Natalie gently swatted the closest bottom. "Now scoot."

"Can Cooper listen, too?" Lily asked. At some point during the evening, she'd become attached to Cooper's side and had budged only for more decorations or popcorn.

"Can I listen, too, Mom?" he teased.

"Only if you promise to be a good boy."

A wicked grin lit his face. For a second she feared he'd say something she would regret. "I have to be. Puppy's in there somewhere."

A trickle of relief had her grinning in return. "Don't you forget it, either. Three girls alone must have a protector." From big bad wolves as well as handsome doctors with killer smiles and fancy cars. "Have another cup of coffee or some cookies. I'll get the girls started and be right back."

When she returned, Cooper was on one knee in her kitchen poking around in her oven. "What's wrong with this?"

"Why do you think anything is?"

"I saw you banging the inside before putting in that pan of cookies."

"Oh." The element acted up sometimes and wouldn't heat without a little whack. "Well, don't get any big ideas. I don't need a new oven." When he only smiled, she pointed at him. "I mean it, Cooper. Don't go there again. If I can't afford it, I don't buy it. I do not want your help, your charity or whatever you call it."

"You take away the joy of living," he said mildly. "If a man can't spend his money, what good is it?"

"Spend it on someone else."

"Make me a list." When she gave him a frustrated look, he shook his head with a smile. "Okay, okay. I'll back off. For now. But if you need anything, I want to know about it."

Oh, sure, like she'd ask a man to take care of her. A sugar daddy. No, thanks. As much fun as Cooper could be, this overblown sense of responsibility was wearing thin.

"Can we talk about something else?" she asked as she led the way back into the crammed living room.

"Anything." He sat down on her couch with all the grace and ease of an athlete. For a man who spent hours in the hospital and many more doing research, he was in remarkably great shape.

"Do you still sail?"

"Every chance I get. Want to go?"

"In the dead of winter?"

"Maybe we'll wait for spring. We could take in the Frog Pond, though, if you're in the mood to ice skate."

"I wasn't asking for a date, Cooper."

With a tight smile he said, "Can't friends go skating together?"

Now she felt like a jerk.

At that moment, the twins reappeared in flannel pjs, all pink and shiny from their baths, green frog slippers flip-flopping on the wooden floors.

They fell against Natalie and she hugged them close, breathing in their clean, little girl scents. Her heart nearly burst with love. "You smell yummy."

"Can we stay up longer?"

Natalie glanced at the wall clock. "Better not if you want a story."

The twins climbed off their mom's lap. "We knew you'd say that. Come on."

"Did you brush your teeth?" She asked as they started down the hall. Both girls nodded.

Lily turned to their visitor. "Come on, Cooper."

He lounged with one arm on the doorpost between the kitchen and living room. "Will I be intruding?"

While the two girls looked at him in bewilderment, Natalie shook her head. "Of course not."

She had moved to this duplex to save money after Justin's death. Now it felt strange having a man enter one of their bedrooms. Not frightening or disconcerting. Just different. Maybe even a good different. She'd have to think about that later.

"I like your room," Cooper said, looking around. The twins' bedroom was decorated in pink and purple according to their tastes, with a bed on each side of the room and a dresser in between.

"We do, too. Mommy made it."

"The entire room?" His admiring gaze found hers. "I'm impressed."

High on the wall above each bed, Natalie had created giant crowns from which hung a pair of white sheer curtains to form a princess canopy. Using fabric, buttons, lace and tassels bought at secondhand stores and garage sales, she and the girls had created fairy princess bedspreads and pillow covers.

"It was fun, wasn't it, girls?" But Cooper's compliment glowed deep down in her belly.

"Cakes, crowns and little girls," Cooper mused. "I don't think I ever realized how talented you are."

"One more compliment and my head will

be too big to fit under the canopy."

By now the twins had each climbed into her own bed. Lily pushed back her filmy canopy and patted the mattress. "Sit here, Cooper."

He looked a little lost for a second but quickly covered. For the first time ever, Natalie wondered if the golden boy who could do anything felt out of his element with two vivacious little girls. If he did, he covered it well, but that tiny moment of uncertainty, instead of offending, touched her heart. The man was human. Vulnerable. Funny how she'd never thought *that* about Cooper Sullivan.

The girls, even Rose, insisted on hearing Cooper read the story of Rudolph. That, too, pierced Natalie. She was certainly feeling mushy and sentimental tonight, but the picture of a brilliant, sophisticated surgeon ho-ho-hoing like Santa was too sweet.

Natalie watched her girls' faces, especially Lily who hung on every word Cooper spoke. Precious Lily was her sensitive one, the child who took cookies to the neighbor and worried about outside dogs getting cold.

A look at Rose reminded her that Rose, too, could be gentle and giving, though in a different way. Where Lily was the peacemaker, Rose wanted to beat up those who mistreated others. Sometimes she wondered if this daughter hadn't been more negatively impacted by the loss of her daddy than the other.

The heaviness tried to seep in but Natalie refused to give way. Tonight had been good for them all. Her children needed to hear a man's voice, to roughhouse and joke in a way only males could do.

After the third story, Natalie leaned down to kiss Rose. "Time to go sleep."

"One more. Please, one more."

Taking his cue, Cooper clapped the book shut and stroked the hair back from Lily's face. "Another time. Okay?"

Natalie's heart bumped against her ribs. Another time? Tonight had been both pleasant and difficult. She wasn't sure she wanted to do this again anytime soon.

"Tomorrow?" Lily was asking. "Will you come tomorrow?"

Natalie kissed each daughter. "Cooper's a busy doctor."

"Oh. Like Daddy was." The small voice sounded sadly accepting. They'd seen so little of their father because of his demanding residency.

"Good night, my angels. I love you."

" 'Night, Mommy."

"And Cooper," Lily said, eager as always

not to leave anyone out. Already, she had six baby dolls lined along her pillow because she worried their feelings would be hurt if she left one in the toy chest.

"Good night," Cooper said from the doorway.

Natalie flipped off the light and headed back into the living room. Cooper walked along next to her.

"Time for me to go, too." He took his coat from the back of the couch and started toward the door. "I have an early case."

"What time?"

"Six."

"Painful."

He smiled, softly. "I'm used to it."

"I know. But it's still painful."

With only the tree lights on, the living room was in pleasant shadow, the magical feel of Christmas in the air.

"That tree needs some gifts under it."

"Don't worry. The girls get plenty."

"Will you let me buy them something?"

"Only if it's small."

"What do they want?"

"What did you want when you were a kid?"

"Everything in sight."

"There you go. But I'm an old-fashioned mom. I don't want my girls to think money buys happiness."

"Wise mom. Your girls are lucky."

Cooper grew quietly pensive. Focused on the sparsely decorated tree behind her, he drew a pair of black leather gloves absently through his tightened fist.

Natalie wondered what kind of childhood Cooper had experienced. Had his Christmases been full of joy, or only full of stuff? She'd always assumed he'd led a charmed life. But what did she really know about him?

She laid a hand on the crook of his elbow. "You made some good memories for my girls tonight. Thank you."

"What about their mom? Did she have fun?" His expression grew serious.

"She did."

"Me, too."

The memory of that surprising kiss rushed in. Why had he done it? Was it only a moment of madness, some macho move to prove a point or something else entirely?

He opened the door and stepped out into the night. The snow had stopped and the air was clear and calm and sweet. Streetlights turned the new snow to diamonds. "We'll have to do it again sometime."

She followed him out, arms folded to ward off the chill. "That's not necessary, Cooper."

He gazed down at her, something unreadable in his dark, dark eyes.

"You'd better go in." But he made no move to leave.

"Yes."

She gave a small, self-conscious laugh. She was a little jittery, standing in the dark with him, her traitorous brain remembering the earlier kiss.

Did he?

Cooper reached up to touch her cheek.

The door behind them opened. Rose stood silhouetted there, a stuffed bunny rabbit tucked beneath one arm. "I'm thirsty."

Cooper dropped his hand. " 'Night, Natalie. Sweet dreams."

Cooper closed the lid on his laptop computer and sat back against the rough fabric of his office chair, rubbing his eyes. It was after two in the morning and he had an early call. He'd been too jazzed to sleep after the evening with Natalie and her girls, and the never-ending research proved a worthy distraction. This time of night was perfect for conversing with surgeons and researchers in other parts of the world.

Quiet, broken only by the infinitesimal hum of the heating unit, filled the darkened town house. He snapped off the office light, stood and stretched, before going into the living room. The enormous white sectional sofa, designer chosen, was visible in the dark. Beyond that was the white stone fireplace he had never used. What was the point? He was never here long enough to enjoy a crackling fire. Besides, what good was a romantic fireplace without someone to share it with?

He'd never been lonely. Tonight — or rather this morning — he was. Must be lack of sleep.

He went to the window, pushed aside the heavy drapes and looked out over the elite neighborhood. This was the kind of place where he'd grown up. Upscale homes filled with prominent families who'd reached the zenith of their respective professions. Most of them born of the New England aristocracy, interested in being seen and appreciated for who they were and what they could do, and always enjoying only the best money could buy. It was, after all, their rightful place in society.

He'd never considered anything else — until now.

Those few hours with Natalie and her girls had done something to him.

How different the simple warmth in her tiny duplex was from his childhood home.

He'd had everything material, and his parents loved him in their own way, but Christmas was a time to showcase the Sullivan prominence and power with elegant dinner parties and visits from all the right people, not a time to laugh and eat popcorn and sing silly songs. Had his mother ever once displayed any of the paper angels or glittered bells he and Cameron had created at school? Natalie would have.

An ache started between his eyes and spread to his throat. Being around Justin's family was both pleasure and pain.

He shouldn't have kissed her. Guilt had gnawed at him all evening. He'd vowed to help Justin's widow, not hit on her.

But here was the worst part. He wasn't sorry. He'd loved kissing her, loved the taste, however brief, of her honey sweetness. For a moment there, he could have sworn she'd been kissing him back, pressing toward him as if he was water and she parched ground. Or maybe it had been the other way around.

If she was anyone on earth except Justin's widow, they could have a fling, maybe even an affair of some length. When it was over, they could both go on, the better for having known each other.

His hand tightened on the windowsill as

he imagined Natalie in this house, in his bed. Yes, a long, luxurious affair in which he showered her with all the things she didn't have and loved her until he was filled.

With a soft curse, he spun away from the window.

She was Natalie, Justin's widow, the marrying kind. And he was a sorry excuse for a friend.

CHAPTER SIX

Three days later, a delivery truck pulled up to Natalie's house bearing a top-of-the-line baker's oven. Natalie didn't let the men unload it. When she tried to phone Cooper, his voice mail picked up. Figuring he was in surgery, she left a message saying "Thanks but no thanks."

She was still ruffled hours later when she stopped by the Wedding Belles' office to pick up her check. As soon as she began spouting her upset to Julie and Audra, guilt set in. She shouldn't unload on either of these friends, considering how preoccupied and anxious they'd both been of late.

The situation with Audra was perfectly understandable. The Belles' accountant hadn't been herself since her jerk fiancé had left her at the altar. Oh, she said she was fine and had carried on, but the Belles all knew better. Add to that the financial strain the business had been under after the Vandiver wedding fiasco and Audra's computer brain couldn't bear the strain.

Then there was Julie, the receptionist, whose crazy laugh and high energy usually filled the office with a daily dose of the unexpected. Lately even she had been strangely quiet as the time for her fantasy wedding grew closer. Jitters, she supposed.

Natalie almost felt guilty for complaining. But she did it, anyway.

"Sugar pie," Belle drawled as she sauntered into the office from her adjoining one. Her belted turquoise tunic and black slacks showed off her ample curves in an understated way. And nobody could wear a silk scarf with the panache of Belle Mackenzie. "Don't look a gift horse in the mouth, especially when he has a million-dollar smile and a bank account to go with it."

"Belle, stop that! You know I would never be interested in a man because of his money. Quite the contrary."

"Well, don't be too contrary about it, honey. There is nothing wrong with a healthy pocketbook." Belle laughed her rich throaty chuckle. "All Southern mamas teach their daughters to follow their hearts but to have the good sense God gave them to keep their eyes open, too. It's just as easy to fall for a rich man as it is as a poor one."

"Is Natalie in love?" Callie came through the doorway carrying a bouquet of white poinsettias. If humming and starry eyes were any indication, the florist's honeymoon was still in high gear.

"No. I am not in love! And I wish people would stop assuming that just because Cooper is incredibly smart and good looking and rich that I have the hots for him."

The newlywed paused, extending a posy. "I fear thou doth protest too much."

Natalie bit back a scream. "I love you ladies, but you are driving me crazy. Cooper Sullivan isn't interested in me."

"Then why did he call here twice yesterday?" asked Belle.

"And send an oven this morning?" Julie pushed at a wad of tight red curls. "Come to think of it. An oven is a weird gift. Not at all romantic."

"Perfectly logical to me," said Audra, who had swiveled back to her computer to tap at the keys.

"He isn't interested in romance, I tell you." Natalie didn't dare tell them about the kiss. They'd all go crazy with speculation. She was having enough trouble forgetting it herself, even though she knew one little kiss to Cooper Sullivan was like one drop of rain to an ocean. Nothing at all.

131

"Could that be why you're so upset?" Belle lowered herself onto a chair next to Audra's desk. "A gorgeous man buys you kitchen appliances instead of diamond rings?"

Natalie looked at her in horror. "Of course not. I don't want anything at all from Cooper. From any man. I can take care of myself."

"We all need a little help now and then, sugar."

"Not you, Belle. You're an independent woman."

Her boss tilted her head and gazed at Natalie, puzzling over something.

"Now don't get your blood sugar in an uproar, Natalie," Callie spoke up. "But did you ever consider that the man may find you attractive? You aren't exactly dog meat."

"Oh, please. I haven't colored my hair in two years. I've forgotten the fine art of flirtation. And I have two kids!"

But he'd kissed her in spite of those things.

Callie waved off her arguments. "Obviously, the man likes kids. He's a pediatric surgeon, for goodness' sake. And you have the kind of pale-blond hair that needs nothing. Even with flower spikes holding it in place."

Natalie grabbed the top of her head. Had

she left those things in there again?

"Why not give your cute doctor a chance?" Julie said over one shoulder as she slid open a file cabinet. "What can it hurt?"

It could hurt a lot, Natalie thought. If she were to put her heart out there again, to take a chance with a man, not knowing his motives, she and the girls could both be badly wounded.

"Callie's right," Belle said. "Christmas is the perfect time for giving, and that man has more Christmas spirit than any that's come along in a while. Even if he is giving kitchen appliances."

Christmas spirit or determination to have his own way?

"More giving than Charlie?" Grinning slyly, Julie slammed the file drawer.

For weeks now, Belle had resisted the attentions of Charles Wiley but all the other women knew it was only a matter of time until sweet Charlie wore down her resistance.

"Charlie is a different matter. I let him kiss me last night." Belle's smile was smug.

Callie slapped Natalie a high-five. They'd had a bet that Belle would soon succumb to the kind and generous Charlie. "The man is crazy about you."

"I know." With a wave of one hand, she

laughed. "All this time I thought he only wanted to buy my vintage Rolls."

"We know what Charlie wants to do in that car."

"Kisses, girls. Kisses. That's all Charlie and I are up to."

The chatter went on, teasing Belle until the conversation switched to business and the upcoming weddings. Natalie was glad the attention had been diverted from her and Cooper. She didn't quite know how to react to his attention, and the Belles weren't helping with their innuendos.

The desk telephone played the wedding march. The room quieted as Julie spoke into the receiver, "Wedding Belles. Julie speaking. How may I help you?"

Her brown eyes flashed to Natalie. She put a hand over the receiver and in a stage whisper that could have been heard at the back of Symphony Hall, she said, "It's him."

"Tell him I'm not here."

Julie looked puzzled. "But you are."

Natalie let her head fall back. She stuck out her hand and took the receiver.

"Hello, Cooper."

"Natalie." The rumbling baritone tickled her ear.

"I sent it back."

He chuckled. "Maybe not." And the phone

134

went dead.

She stood staring at the silent telephone until four pairs of eyes forced her to look up.

"Well?" Callie insisted, hand on hip. "What was that all about?"

"I have no idea." Which wasn't exactly true, but she didn't know what else to tell them. "Look, are we going to work on ideas for Julie's wedding or not?"

She whipped toward the receptionist, eager to escape the thunder in her veins and the sound of Cooper's sexy voice hinting at mischief. "Julie, I brought some new designs to show you. You said you'd always dreamed of a more whimsical wedding cake. What do you think of this?"

"Oh." Julie's fingers fluttered to her lips. "Natalie, you shouldn't have."

Ignoring the protest, Natalie opened the sketch book and shared her ideas. All the Belles were excited about helping Julie and Matt have their dream wedding. Julie protested sweetly, but they knew she wanted this as much as they wanted to do it for her.

When Callie added her thoughts on the perfect flowers for the bouquet and tables, everyone momentarily lost interest in harassing Natalie. Julie was such a great girl who was always doing something to help someone else. In fact, she had invested every penny of her savings to bolster her fiancé's struggling business. When the other Belles got wind of her sacrifice, they'd chipped in to throw Julie the wedding of the year.

"You are all so sweet for wanting to do this for Matt and me," Julie said, worrying her bottom lip. "I kind of feel bad about causing so much trouble."

"Trouble?" Belle said, giving Julie's shoulders a hug. "Honey, this is pure pleasure. If we can't give one of our own a spectacular wedding, we should just give it up and go out of business."

Audra shot their boss a troubled glance. Natalie made a mental note to ask her later if something was wrong. The accountant was jittery today.

"Are we having a meeting I don't know about?"

All eyes turned to the company photographer. Regina, in long gray coat and pink, high-heeled boots, brought in the scent of cold outdoors. Her cheeks glowed, her eyes were wide and dewy, and her expression was excited.

"Wow," said Julie. "You look . . . different." Her voice trailed off as she grappled for the right description.

Regina did look different. With a smile as

wide as the Charles River, she unbuttoned her coat and pushed back the sides.

"What do you think, Belles?" She tilted back and framed her belly with both hands. "Do I look like a mama to you?"

Natalie bolted out of her chair. "Regina O'Ryan! Are you pregnant? Why didn't you tell me? Oh, this is awesome. What does Dell think? Is he the happiest man on the planet?"

Regina beamed. "He is so proud of himself. You'd think he was the only man who'd ever procreated."

"From the smile on your face every morning, I'd say he does a good job."

Everyone chortled as the other Belles gathered around their pregnant coworker. "How far along are you? I can't tell a thing."

"Three months. I wanted to be sure before . . ." She let the words trail off. They all knew she'd miscarried a baby and nearly lost her marriage in the aftermath.

Belle pulled her close for a warm hug. "Everything is going to be fine this time, sugar. You and Dell will have the healthiest baby in Boston."

"That's because the rest of us will nag and coddle you."

Regina laughed. "Along with Dell. He's already ordered me to cut back my hours."

"Don't you adore a man who knows when to take charge?" Belle asked.

"Not particularly," Natalie said without thinking. When all eyes turned to stare, she said, "Never mind. Forget I said that. Dell loves Regina. He can be bossy if he wants to."

"Right," Regina laughed. "As long as I don't have to pay any attention."

"But you will listen to us," Audra said, coming out from behind her desk. "Those shoes are not at all sensible for a pregnant woman."

Regina stretched her back. "Believe me, I figured that out on the subway."

"Dell let you take the subway?"

"Shh. Dell does not know everything."

They were all still exclaiming over the baby-to-be and had begun to plan a future baby shower when a burly man in a green uniform entered the room.

"One of you ladies Natalie Thompson?"

"Oh, Lord," Audra whispered. "What has Rose done now?"

Natalie shot her a quelling look and then said to the man, "I'm Natalie."

He extended an invoice. "All set up just the way you ordered."

Slowly, Natalie accepted the document. "I didn't order anything."

"Well, somebody did."

And she knew who. "Take it back."

She pushed the invoice toward him, but the workman stepped back, both hands raised. "Lady, me and the fellas spent three hours installing that oven in your itty-bitty kitchen. There is no way in Hades — pardon my French — that we are taking that thing out."

Before she could say another word, he turned on his boot heel and left.

"This is impossible." Dumbstruck, she stared down at the sheet of paper declaring her the owner of the baker's oven she'd returned just this morning. "They can't go into my house and install an oven without my permission. I'm calling the police."

"Oh, come on, Natalie. Get real." Julie slammed a desk drawer with more than a little force. "The man is trying to help you."

"You need that oven, girlfriend." Callie tapped her with a calla lily. "The last cake samples were a little dry."

Natalie gasped. Her cakes were her livelihood. If the old oven let her down, what would she do?

With a sinking feeling, she knew the answer. She'd accept the new oven for the sake of her children. But she would also let Cooper know exactly what she thought about his high-handed attitude.

Natalie left her van in the Newbury Street parking garage and took the T straight to Cooper's office on Longwood Avenue. Today was the day to get this straight, once and for all.

"I need to see Dr. Sullivan, please," she said to the scrub-clad woman behind the window.

"Your name?" The receptionist, whose badge read Terri, scanned a clipboard, pen at ready.

"Natalie Thompson."

The scanning ceased. Terri gazed at her from behind narrow glasses with unabashed curiosity. "Just a moment please."

Leaving Natalie to wonder if she still had flower spikes in her hair, Terri exited the desk and disappeared into the back. As she did so, several other nurses glanced in Natalie's direction but kept on working. Stewing over exactly how she'd get her point across to a man who didn't know the meaning of *no,* she gazed around the child-oriented waiting room. It was crowded, mostly with mothers and small children. At a bright-yellow table, a thin boy connected to oxygen played quietly with a puzzle while other children played with soft vinyl blocks.

The sight wrenched Natalie's heart, a reminder of how healthy her own children were.

Along one wall a huge aquarium attracted a few other kids. Bright-blue fish darted among the bubbles and seaweed. She couldn't help but smile. Cooper really did have fish for pets. Rose and Lily would love that.

A side door opened and there stood Cooper. Natalie's stomach fluttered inappropriately. In a lab coat open over a gray dress shirt, Cooper strode toward her. She tried not to think about that kiss.

"Natalie, what a surprise."

Yes, she was certain her sudden appearance in his office was a big surprise. The reason for her presence shouldn't be.

"Cooper," she said, sternly, drawing up to her full height of almost five feet.

"Uh-oh, Doc." Someone in the waiting room chuckled. "You're in trouble with the missus."

Natalie turned to tell the man in no uncertain terms that she was not anyone's missus, but Cooper caught her arm and propelled her down the hallway to his office. He settled her into a plush chair and pulled another next to hers.

"Did you like my present?"

141

His dark eyes sparkled. She wondered if the excitement originated from the gift giving or because he'd managed to outmaneuver her.

"No." She shifted. "Well, yes, I liked it but —"

"Good. I knew you would. The man at the appliance store said it was the best one money could buy."

"Cooper, that's not the point. I asked you not to buy me things. Please. It's embarrassing." More like terrifying. She didn't need another high-rolling man to run her life. Especially when he smelled so good and looked even better.

"I never meant to embarrass you." A furrow creased his forehead. "But the old oven had to go. Justin would want you to have the best."

Justin? He had done this for Justin?

She blinked.

Oh.

Now things were starting to make sense. And she felt more liked chopped liver than ever.

"I can't repay you for an oven of that caliber and you know it."

The frown disappeared and darned if his sexy bottom lip didn't tilt upward. "Consider it a Christmas gift."

She sighed. They were getting exactly nowhere. Worse than nowhere. She was noticing him far too much. When his knee brushed her thigh, she nearly jumped out of the chair.

"Look Natalie," he said, moving close enough to make her stomach dive straight to the toes of her shoes. "I've seen how hard you work. You're good at what you do. You have talent and ambition and smarts. What's wrong with a friend investing in that?"

With every word of affirmation, Natalie's resolve softened. He'd noticed her talent? Justin had laughed at her. He'd considered her dream of running her own business to be cute and sweet but never smart. In fact, Justin had always been the smart one in the family. Not her.

She'd believed in herself because she'd had no other choice. Cooper's encouragement was like balm to a wound.

How could she object after that? Besides, she had little choice in the matter. Mr. Burly wasn't going to take the oven back and she couldn't afford to pay someone else to remove it.

"Okay," she said, trying to hide the pleasure. "But please don't do it again."

Gee, wasn't she the tough one?

"So when are you going to bake a cake for

me?" The tilted lips became a full-blown smile.

Natalie let the pleasure out, returning the warm smile. "I came here to give you a piece of my mind, not a piece of cake."

"Does that mean my sparkling personality has won you over, and I can set up trust funds for the girls?"

"Cooper," she sighed, shaking her head.

Why was helping her so important to him? Could it really just be because of his friendship with Justin?

Callie's teasing echoed in her head. She wanted to ask Cooper straight-out if he was interested in her as a woman or because she was Justin's needy widow. But she'd been embarrassed enough for one day.

Worse yet, she didn't know which answer she preferred.

His compliments glowed inside her like a candle in a window on a snowy night. She focused on the feeling, reliving the pleasure. Then the room faded and she felt herself floating away.

"Natalie," Cooper's voice came from a distance. "Have you had lunch? Your hands are shaking."

She looked down. Her hands *were* shaking, and so were her insides. The floating wasn't pleasure, it was insulin shock. Rally-

144

ing, she dug into her handbag. "I have some candy in here somewhere."

"Do you do this often? Forget to eat?"

"No. Well, sometimes when I'm really busy or distracted." Dandy. Now Cooper would have more reason to think she was a helpless female in need of a man to run her life.

She found a piece of hard candy and popped it into her mouth.

Cooper stood and held out a hand. "Come on. Have lunch with me."

"Don't you have patients?"

"Doctors on staff at this facility get to eat at least once a week. It's a perk of our superiority."

"Really, I'm okay. Don't worry. I'll grab something on my way home." Avoiding his hand, she rose, purse clutched in front of her like a shield. Thank goodness her knees were steady.

Cooper studied her for a nanosecond. "I really don't like the idea of you driving around Boston in this condition."

His choice of words scraped her nerves like fingernails on a chalkboard. She didn't bother to tell him she'd taken the subway. "I'm an adult, Cooper, perfectly able to make my own decisions."

"It was a lunch invitation, Natalie, not a

145

request for power of attorney. I'm concerned. Is that such a bad thing?"

"I —" Was she really so neurotic that she couldn't have lunch with a man she liked just because he'd bought her an oven? How messed up was that? She sighed in defeat. "Okay. Lunch. One lunch."

That devilish grin wreathed his face.

She laughed in spite of herself. Infuriating, charming and funny. A woman could fall for a guy like that.

At the thought, her brain, already low on sugar, stopped working altogether. She was not about to fall in love with anybody, certainly not an overachieving surgeon with some misguided sense of duty to her late husband.

But she could have lunch.

CHAPTER SEVEN

"No worries," Cooper said to the white-faced parents as he walked beside their child's gurney toward the operating room. "She'll do fine."

IV tubing thudded softly against the metal railing and paper surgical booties swished against the tile. The familiar medicine smell filled Cooper's nostrils. For today's modern surgeons, the nine-year-old's surgery was about as routine as they got. Nevertheless, he'd spent extra time last night going over every detail, remapping a computer model of the girl's heart and studying the latest lab and scan results. They were as ready as humanly possible.

One of the scrub-clad nurses patted the mother's arm. "You've got the best team of surgeons in the country. Everything should go perfectly."

Giving the worried mother and dad a wink and a cocky smile, Cooper said, "This one's a piece of cake."

The phrase made him think of Natalie and his smile widened. The parents grinned back as if the action was meant for them. Whatever calmed them down. They had no need to worry with him at the helm.

He entered the scrub area and began his preparations while nurses and doctors prepped the patient. As he scrubbed the soft brush up and down his arms, his mind stayed on Natalie. She'd seemed to soften up some after the oven episode. They'd had a nice lunch, which had amazingly become daily lunches filled with conversation that was both stimulating and fun. Each day he returned to his office energized and looking forward to more.

Work had kept him from taking her to dinner, but that was next on his agenda.

Completing the scrub, he exchanged the brush for a sterile towel and then his surgical gown. A nurse held a pair of latex gloves. He pushed his skilled hands into them and felt the familiar snap against his skin. The usual hum of efficient professionals and surgical machines ebbed around him.

He liked being with Natalie. Once, a long time ago for a brief time, he'd been interested in her. Now, with Justin gone, wanting to be with her felt wrong, as if he'd somehow wished his friend dead. Yet he couldn't seem to help himself. It was as if he had to see her. Sometimes he was worried it had nothing to do with loyalty to Justin and everything to do with Natalie.

"Dr. Sullivan, we're ready to begin."

He looked up. His team of scrub techs and physicians watched him. Shaking off all thoughts of Natalie, he stepped to the table.

For the next few hours, he was completely focused. A small heart and lungs filled his gifted hands and mind. The hush-swoosh of the heart-lung machine kept a steady rhythm with the beats and ticks of a dozen monitors. The little girl was doing well.

And then something went terribly wrong. Suddenly, for no reason any of them could fathom, the child's blood pressure collapsed. Cooper's pulse accelerated. He was not going to lose her. He would not fail. She was nine years old, for God's sake, all bubble and bounce and smiley-faced balloons. She'd trusted him to make her well.

He labored hard and long, pulling out every trick he'd ever learned and a few he invented on the spot.

"Dr. Sullivan." Someone put a hand on his arm. He kept working. "Cooper. You have to call it."

He stepped back, all the energy draining

out of him, and looked at the clock. "Time of death, 3:47 p.m."

As always after a loss, the surgical suite was strangely silent, broken only by the hush-swoosh of inanimate machines that did not know they were now useless.

Stanching the stinging disappointment, he stripped away bloody gloves, slammed his foot onto the trash can pedal, and let the lid fall with a bang. Failure lay like a brick in his gut.

Abruptly he turned on his heel, composed his expression and went to break the devastating news to the waiting parents. He'd gone into the OR believing he was a god of medicine. Fate had a way of making him pay for such foolish thoughts.

Arms loaded down with groceries and Christmas gifts, Natalie kicked the front door closed with the flat of her foot. This afternoon had been the perfect time for shopping without the girls, since they were attending a friend's birthday sleep-over. She would have time to wrap everything and then take a long leisurely soak in the tub without some munchkin banging on the door.

Ah, the small joys of motherhood.

After putting away the groceries, she

spread the presents out on a table for wrapping. Both Rose and Lily loved to playact, so she was creating a costume trunk by decorating an old trunk in the grand style of 1930s movie stars and filling it with thrift shop and dollar store dress-up items. They really wanted a trampoline, but it wasn't happening this year.

She rolled out a length of bright red and green paper just as the doorbell chimed.

One peek through the security hole and her heart bumped. She yanked the door open with more pleasure than was prudent. "Cooper, hi. Come in."

Immediately she recognized his mood. Gone were his "I'm hot" smile and his cocky king-of-the-universe aura. "Is something wrong?"

"Bad day at the office."

"I'm sorry."

"Yeah. Maybe I should just go. I don't know why I came over here. I'll be lousy company."

She grabbed the sleeve of his jacket. He wasn't going anywhere if she had any say in it. Something bad had occurred. She'd seen Justin like this a few times, not often, but she knew it happened. Even doctors had feelings.

"Want to talk about it?"

He let out a gusty sigh as if he'd been holding his breath, hoping she'd offer. "Do you mind?"

"Sit. I'll get coffee. Are you hungry?"

He shook his head. "Coffee's good for now."

She set the mugs in front of him and joined him on the sofa. In the tiny living quarters, a sofa was it. She brought a knee up and turned to face him. "What happened?"

And so he told her about a little girl who should have made it but hadn't. A child who had died on his table.

Her throat clogged with emotion. Cooper was a trained, objective surgeon. She knew from watching Justin that doctors learned to turn off that part of the brain that grieves too hard at a loss. For some reason, this child had slipped beneath Cooper's protective shield.

"You did everything in your power to save her." She knew this without asking. It was simply the way Cooper was.

"Yeah. I just can't figure out what went wrong. Afterward, I went over all the tests, the consults, everything." He scrubbed a hand down his face. Whiskers scraped over normally smooth skin. "There was no medical reason. None. Her body just gave out."

"It wasn't meant to be, Cooper. Sometimes you have to accept that."

They talked on, and Natalie heard the heart, not of the doctor, but of the man. She hadn't realized the overconfident Cooper was so deeply compassionate, that he cared so much. It was a disconcerting revelation.

"You've lost patients before. Why did this one hit you so hard?"

He paused, sipped his coffee, and then slanted her a look. "Rose and Lily."

Natalie frowned. "What?"

"She was a petite little blonde with big eyes and a sassy grin, so full of life. I liked her. She reminded me of them. I felt like I'd lost one of your girls."

"Oh, Cooper." Natalie wrapped her arms around him and laid her head on his shoulder. "I'm so sorry."

Cooper responded by pulling her close, his upset heavy between them. For the longest time they sat together in an embrace of comfort. Natalie rubbed her hand up and down his back as she'd done to comfort her girls a hundred times. She didn't mind at all that her work wasn't getting done, the gifts weren't being wrapped and no cakes were cooking in the oven.

Cooper needed her tonight.

Finally he pulled back and cleared his throat, expression slightly chagrined. "Sorry."

"Don't be. It's okay to have feelings. In fact, I like you better because of it."

A slight smile pulled at his gorgeous face. "Thanks for listening. I don't usually whine."

"That wasn't whining, so stop apologizing."

"I guess I should go." But he made no move to do so.

She pushed off the couch. "Why don't you stay? We'll make some hamburgers, and you can help me wrap these gifts."

"You live dangerously if you think I can wrap anything. Sew a button, yes. Wrap a gift, no way."

"Life's an adventure," she said lightly, glad to see him teasing again. It felt good to know she'd cheered him up, at least a little. It felt even better to realize Cooper Sullivan was vulnerable, human. The notion was a little scary, too. The better she knew him, the more she liked him.

And that wasn't a good thing. Was it?

After that night Natalie was a mess. Somehow in the space of that one evening, her opinion of Cooper had changed.

Since then, she'd seen him every day, sometimes twice. And even though her brain said the action was unwise, the rest of her went right on enjoying his company.

Intellectually she was convinced his attentions were all because of Justin. He'd told her often enough he was not in the market for a relationship. He only wanted to help his old buddy's family the way Justin would expect.

And yet, when they were together, Justin was the furthest thing from her mind.

She was in trouble. Real trouble.

She was decorating a cake — what else? — when even more trouble began. The telephone rang. In the middle of creating a cascade of burgundy roses, she yelled, "Will one of you get the phone, please?"

The ringing stopped and she heard the murmur of Rose's voice.

"Who was it?" she asked when the murmuring ceased.

Rose ambled into the kitchen and peered at the glass-enclosed sampler tray. "Nobody."

"Telemarketer?"

Her daughter shrugged. "I guess so. Can I have a piece of red velvet cake?"

"How about an apple?"

Her daughter made a face but accepted

the inevitable. Cake was everywhere, but access was limited to all members of the Thompson household. Occasionally Natalie created a diabetic dessert but most times opted for fruit as the healthier choice.

"Mom?"

"Hmm?"

Rose crunched into the Red Delicious. "Never mind."

The dejected tone caught Natalie's attention. "Is everything okay?"

"Do you still love Daddy?"

Natalie squeezed one more flower onto the cake and placed the pastry bag to one side to study her child. How did a mother explain that life had to go on? That love wouldn't bring Justin back?

"Of course I do, baby. We'll always love Daddy. Why do you ask such a thing?"

"Lily wants you to marry Cooper so we can have a new daddy."

A piece of Natalie's heart broke off. Lily had made her adulation of Cooper clear to everyone, including Cooper. She longed for a father figure in her life in the same way Rose protected Justin's memory with the ferocity of a mother bear.

"Nothing can take away your memories of Daddy. He was a good daddy, he loved you, and nothing will ever change that."

The hedge wasn't lost on a smart cookie like Rose. "But some kids get new daddies."

"There's nothing wrong with that, sweetheart."

Tears glistened in Rose's eyes. "Please don't marry Cooper."

"Cooper and I are just friends." Anyway she was still telling herself that.

"I think he likes you more than friends."

What did an eight-year-old know of such things? Could she sense the zing in her mother's blood whenever Cooper stood close or laughed his sexy laugh?

"Come here, Rosie-posy," she said, drawing her child against her body. Rose buried her face in her mother's side. "I like Cooper. He was your daddy's friend. It's okay if you like him, too. Daddy wouldn't mind."

When Rose sighed and clung a bit tighter, Natalie thought she was getting somewhere.

She'd thought wrong.

"I don't like him," Rose announced.

Then she flounced out of the kitchen.

Natalie looked at the ceiling and exhaled an exasperated breath. While one twin quietly dressed dolls and read fairy tales, the other talked to an invisible pit bull and snitched frosting and cake when no one was looking.

The timer on the new commercial oven

went off just as the doorbell chimed. Though still getting used to all the bells and whistles, Natalie loved the precision and versatility of the new machine. Cooper bought only the best. As hard as she tried to be mad at him for buying the oven, she loved it. Checking the raspberry torte, she found it not quite done, and reset the timer before going to the door.

Cooper, looking harried and hurried and utterly gorgeous, stood on her porch. "Thank heavens you're here. Is something wrong?"

She blinked twice, uncomprehending. "Everything's fine. Why?"

"One of the twins told me you weren't home. Scared me to death to think they were home alone. I thought something had happened to you in that old van. The diabetes . . ."

Uh-oh. "I've been here with the girls all evening."

A sneaking suspicion gathered at the back of her brain. Surely not. Surely Rose would not tell an outright lie.

She stepped back to let him in. "Did you call a while ago? Maybe twenty minutes?"

He nodded. Natalie's suspicion became a certainty. She closed her eyes to count to ten. At five, she yelled, "Rose Isabella!"

Cooper's blood was still pounding in his ears after the wild drive from Cambridge to Natalie's duplex in Dorchester. He'd had visions of a terrible accident or a diabetic collapse, knowing only an emergency could cause Natalie to leave her children untended. His insides still trembled.

Rose slunk into the living room, saw Cooper and spun as if to leave.

"Stay right there, little miss." Natalie's soft voice held iron. "I think you have some explaining to do."

"I didn't know it was him. I promise."

The little monkey.

Natalie's voice was firm. "Rose, that's not true and we both know it. Telling lies is wrong and will always get you in trouble. I am so disappointed."

Though her face was sullen, Rose said, "I'm sorry, Cooper."

Cooper didn't think she was, but he kept quiet.

Natalie, looking too cute with a pair of glitter pens holding her hair in place, pointed toward the back of the house. "Go take a bath right now and go to bed."

"But tonight's *Frosty*."

"I'm sorry about that, but you are not going to watch television at all for the next two nights. You are grounded."

Rose's sullen face became incredulous. "But all the Christmas shows are on this week."

"You should have thought of that before you told a lie."

"You are the meanest mom ever!" Rose stomped out of the room and shut her bedroom door with a little more effort than necessary.

Natalie slid onto the couch, forehead against her hands. "I'm sorry, Cooper. I don't know what to do with her sometimes."

"You're doing fine, Nat." He'd watched her with the twins enough to know she was great mother, though Rose could be a brat sometimes. "Every parent hits bumps in the road."

Not that he knew much about parenting, but as a pediatrician he'd studied plenty of child psychology and observed his share of kids in action.

"Yeah, well this is a major bump. Rose thinks you're trying to take Justin's place."

Hearing his inner worry spoken aloud, his heart thumped against his rib cage. Since the night she'd listened and fed him hamburgers, he'd been struggling uphill. His

160

motives were pure. He was sure of it. Taking care of her was his responsibility now, but he hadn't expected to enjoy having her take care of him for a change.

"Nobody can take Justin's place," he said, gruffly.

"You're nice to say so." She gave him a tremulous smile, and he had a bad feeling she might get teary on him. "Justin wasn't perfect. He was just a man. A man who made mistakes and left messes he didn't clean up."

"But you loved him, anyway. The two of you were great together." Which was one of the reasons he'd taken a residency in California, though he hadn't realized it until now. Seeing Justin and Natalie together had bothered him. He didn't know why, except that Justin had never beaten him at anything else, even the game of love, though Cooper liked to think he wasn't that shallow anymore.

Maybe he was, because the need to make things right for Natalie grew stronger every time they were together. It couldn't be love since he had no intention of getting that involved with anyone. At least not for a long time. Not until he was made chief. As he well knew, relationships and medical careers seldom went well together. More than half of his colleagues were already divorced at least once.

So, why he couldn't get his mind off Justin Thompson's widow baffled him.

"He thought he had all the time in the world to be a dad to the girls," Natalie was saying, "to make a lot of money, to do all the things we dreamed of. He was under so much pressure in his residency. I didn't want to add to that. But sometimes . . ."

He moved closer. She seemed fragile tonight, not at all the spunky, independent Natalie he'd spent the last few days laughing with. Everything in him wanted to touch her, to comfort her as she'd done for him.

"Sometimes what?" he asked softly.

"Sometimes I wanted him to quit, to be here with us more. To be the strong parent Rose needs. I feel guilty when I think such things because he worked so hard." Tears filled her eyes. "Mostly I'm mad at him. Is that dumb or what?"

"Not dumb at all. I feel the same."

She blinked up, tears trembling on her lashes. "You do?"

"Sure. Nobody pushed me as hard as Justin. He should still be here giving me a hard time." He should also be here with his wife and kids.

Her smile was sad. "You have no idea how

many all-nighters Justin burned because he wanted to get the top score on an exam."

His chuckle was a little sad, too. "I was doing the same thing."

"He burned himself out. Don't you see? He wanted to do it all and have it all, never understanding that it was impossible. He pushed too hard. Worked horrid hours and still tried to squeeze in time for me, the girls, his bike, sailing, building us the perfect house, the perfect life." Hands clenching and unclenching on her lap, Natalie's voice choked into silence.

The need to hold her won out. Gently he pulled her into his arms. With a sigh filled with weariness, she pressed her cheek against his chest. He wondered if she could feel the sudden pounding of his heart, the heavy longing in him to take away the past two years of sorrow.

Slowly her arms slid around his neck and her breath puffed soft and warm through the cotton fiber of his shirt. He gathered her closer still, listening to the tiny gulps that said she was holding back tears.

"It's okay to cry, baby," he whispered.

As if she'd been waiting for permission, quiet sobs shook her shoulders.

He rocked her back and forth, back and forth, trying to absorb her hurt, to take away her sadness.

In the back of the house he heard the children moving around and inhaled the warm scent of ever-present baking. But the sense most affected at the moment rested somewhere deep inside him.

At last the weeping ceased and still she rested against him. He was glad. Natalie carried a heavy load for such a tiny woman. He would stay here on her old slipcovered sofa and hold her all night if necessary.

The idea had more merit than he had a right to consider.

As he did on a daily basis now, Cooper wrestled with the ethics of it all. He had to be here to help Natalie. He knew that for certain. But wanting to kiss her and make love to her had to be way out of line, immoral even. Didn't it?

She stirred, and Cooper dipped his head to look in her eyes. Even red-rimmed, the baby blues did funny things to him. Some of her soft hair had struggled lose from the glitter pens and clung to the moisture on her cheeks. He gently lifted the curl and brushed it away. She was so soft and warm in his arms.

As if he couldn't help himself, Cooper bent to kiss away the tears lingering on her eyelids. She sighed.

"Cooper," she whispered.

He tilted his head in question.

"Kiss me."

His heart jump-started. Oh, man. How could he say no to that?

Cupping the sides of her face, he smiled down. She smiled back. The tiny tremble on her lips, puffy from crying, was more than he could bear.

Ever so gently, he pressed his mouth to hers.

The taste of her was like nothing he'd ever encountered. Like joy and homecoming and healing. When he started to pull back, a little frightened of what was happening inside, Natalie's small hands held him fast. With a tiny sound that set him ablaze, she returned the kiss.

If he'd been standing, he would have gone to his knees.

He kissed her with a tenderness that surprised him, slowly leaning her back against the couch cushions. All the things he wanted to do to her and for her and with her crowded out every other thought. In that moment Natalie became his world.

So when the oven buzzer sounded, he couldn't recognize the source.

"Cooper, my cake." Natalie's voice sounded as ragged as his thoughts.

"Cake?" he was perusing a particular tasty section of her neck. No cake could be better than this.

She pushed at him, her laugh self-conscious. "I have a cake in the oven."

"Oh." Coming out of his fog, he helped her sit upright. That's when he realized they had an audience.

Rose and Lily, wide-eyed and silent, stared at them from the hallway.

Natalie recovered first. She shot into the kitchen, clattering pans and making nervous noises to rescue the great-smelling cake.

Cooper remained behind, wondering what to say to the two puzzled little faces. Well, one was puzzled. The other looked furious, and he suspected the notorious Puppy would appear at any moment.

Rose, eyes squinted, stormed at her mother. "You said you weren't getting married."

"Rose, we'll discuss this later."

"You told me a lie. You said it was bad to lie but you did it, too."

Okay, that was enough for him. He pushed off the couch and went into the kitchen. "Rose, you shouldn't talk to you mother that way."

The little tiger turned on him. "Puppy's going to bite you. You'd better go home."

166

Cooper looked to Natalie, expecting her to take control of the situation. Certainly Rose was upset, but she was also being disrespectful. To his way of thinking, one was acceptable. The other wasn't.

"Natalie?"

The woman he'd been kissing three minutes ago wouldn't meet his gaze.

She fiddled with an oven mitt.

Disappointment made him terse. "Perhaps I should leave."

"Yes. Maybe so." The words hurt.

Stiffly he took his coat from the back of the couch and went to the door, waiting for her to say something more. When she didn't, he said, "You're a person, too."

She only nodded.

One hand on the doorknob, he stared at her for a long moment.

Lily, who'd hung back during Rose's tirade rushed forward. "I like you, Cooper. You're nice."

With a lump in his throat, he patted her cheek and stepped out into the cold night, closing the door behind him.

For a long moment he stood on Natalie's porch and listened to the night sounds around him. A car puttered by. A tree creaked and groaned with the weight of snow. A door slammed. Inside, he heard the murmur of Natalie's voice.

What in the world had happened in there?

A weird sort of electricity rippled through him. Natalie had cried her widow's grief on his shoulder, then kissed him as though he was more than a friend. She still loved Justin. That much was clear. Only, now Cooper wasn't comfortable with leaving things alone as he had ten years ago.

Natalie didn't know what had come over her, but for the first time in two years, she felt like something besides a provider for her children. She felt like a woman.

She touched her lips, still puffy and aching from the kiss that had gone on and on until she'd wanted to push Cooper down on the couch and make crazy, passionate love with him.

Then the twins had appeared. She'd never been so dismayed in her life. For an hour after Cooper's departure, she'd tried to explain the unexplainable to her children. They were too young to understand that their mother was a human being with needs and desires and emotions.

She shook her head and leaned into the mirror. Was she losing her mind? Or finally getting it back from the black abyss of grief?

Poor Cooper. She shouldn't have let him

leave that way. Not when he'd held her so tenderly and listened to her cry.

The house was quiet now. The twins in bed. The cakes cooling on racks or resting in sealed containers.

Natalie remained awake, her blood still humming, her mind still racing and confused.

Closing the bedroom door, she reached for the telephone and dialed Cooper's cell.

He answered on the first ring. "Natalie?"

"I'm sorry."

"For?" His tone was cool, reserved.

"Letting you go." She lay back on the bed. "I was embarrassed. I didn't know what to do."

"I understand."

"Do you?"

"I'm trying to. Rose can't run your life, Natalie."

"I know. I've talked to her." She hoped talking was enough. "I'm sorry I let her behave that way. She's so difficult sometimes, but she's also hurting and confused. She adored Justin and hungered for his company." No need to say Rose's hunger had never been satisfied.

"I'm not trying to take Justin's place."

Was she disappointed to hear him say that?

"Thank you for being a good listener."

"Was that all I was?"

She touched her lips again, imagined him there. "You know the answer to that."

"I wish I were kissing you right now. You taste incredible."

The sexy connotation sent a delicious thrill through her bones. "What's happening between us, Cooper?"

"Not sure. Want to go with it and find out?"

A curl of happiness rose like scented candle smoke. "That's what I was thinking."

CHAPTER EIGHT

"Did you sleep with him?" Regina's eyes, bright with speculation, watched Natalie across the table in Callie's dining room. They were gathered with the other Belles for their Friday-night poker game and girls' night out.

"Regina. Get real. I have two daughters." Who were now playing at a friend's house.

"Want me to invite them for a sleep-over?"

Natalie laughed. Her friends were incorrigible. Sweet but a little goofy. "No, I do not. You know how I feel about sex outside of marriage."

The word *marriage* hung in the air for a full fifteen seconds before either of them spoke again. Regina's mouth formed a speculative *O.* Natalie didn't even want to go there.

"They've already caught us in a compromising situation that I found quite difficult to explain to eight-year-old minds."

171

Julie leaned forward, a salacious grin on her impish face. "Compromising?"

"Necking on the couch," she admitted, her cheeks growing warm.

Callie sauntered in from the kitchen, carrying a tray of margaritas. "Naked on the couch? Natalie, how delicious."

"Not naked. Necking." But she could well have been naked if the twins hadn't been in the house. Very scary thought, that.

"Well, necking is a good start." Callie looked around the table. "Where's Serena? Wasn't she supposed to bring the pizza?"

Cards rippled through Julie's fingers as she shuffled over and over again while waiting for the players to assemble. "Audra's bringing the pizza."

"But it's Serena's turn."

"Haven't you heard?"

"Heard what?" Callie's vermillion mouth pursed in question.

"Serena is the one naked on the couch. Or at least she should be. She called from Lake Tahoe. She and Kane got married last night."

"Married? Why, that little minx. She didn't say a word to me. I'm so mad. I wanted to do her wedding bouquet."

"And I had the perfect cake all picked out," Natalie said. "I even brought samples."

Callie brightened. "Thank goodness. We can have her cake for dessert, with or without her. Now what's this about you and the delicious Cooper Sullivan? If he's after your body, why aren't you with him tonight instead of here with us?"

She didn't bother to correct her friend's assumption that Cooper would automatically want to spend all his time with her. "He's working. A late surgery and on call all night."

Callie settled the tray in the center of the table and pulled up a chair. "I feel your pain. Jared went to a conference this weekend."

"You should have told us. We could have moved the poker game to my house so you could go with him."

Callie waved off the idea. "I love it when he goes on those overnight things."

"Callie!" Such talk from a newlywed shocked them all.

Callie's eyes danced. "Girls, none of you is married yet except Regina, of course. But let me tell you, when Jared is away from me all night, he comes home in a very romantic mood, if you get my drift. No one could have more imaginative ways of getting reacquainted than my red-hot husband." She gave an exaggerated shiver of pleasure.

While all of them giggled, Callie placed a frosty salt-rimmed glass in front of each Belle. "Virgin for you, Regina."

Regina grinned from ear to ear. "Baby and I thank you."

"Sugar-free for our cake fairy." She plopped the frosty glass in front of Natalie. "And the rest of us can get as loopy and fat as we please." She rubbed her palms together. "Now let's get this show on the road. I plan to win back all my quarters tonight."

"And we can discuss plans for Julie's wedding," Regina said. "Did you see the dress Serena's making?"

Callie nodded. "Belle said something about press coverage, too."

"Wow." Excitement rippled around the table. "Julie, this is going to be the most awesome wedding the Belles have ever thrown."

Julie's fingers tensed on the deck of cards. "You gals are amazing," she said, oddly quiet for the vivacious Aussie. "Wonder what's keeping Audra?"

"You don't suppose she's eloped, too?" Callie was in a silly mood tonight.

"With who?" Julie asked, ruffling the cards once again.

"True." Next to Natalie, Audra was the last one to hold out. She wasn't even seeing

174

anyone. "Knowing Audra, she's stuck at the office, poring over the books in an attempt to find one missing penny."

They had a good chuckle at the absent Audra's expense, knowing she wouldn't mind. She was a perfectionist and proud of it.

"There are five of us. Let's play a hand until she gets here."

Natalie held two aces and two deuces when her cell phone chirped. She pushed a quarter into the growing pile with one hand while fishing in her pocket with the other.

Five minutes later she tossed in her cards for good.

"Sorry all. I have to go. Rose is crying with a tummy ache."

"I don't think she was sick at all."

Natalie sat across from Cooper at a small lunch café a few blocks from his office. Somehow it felt natural now to talk things out with him. "Either that or she experienced a miraculous recovery as soon as I arrived."

Natalie didn't mention the rest of the story. That Rose had somehow assumed Natalie was with Cooper instead of playing poker with the Belles. And that her sickness appeared to be a ploy to break up the non-

175

existent date.

"What are you going to do about it?" Cooper asked.

"I don't know." When Cooper raised both eyebrows, she said, "Counseling maybe? I took them both to a grief counselor a few times after Justin's accident. Maybe those few times weren't enough." She constantly tried to second-guess the decisions she made about the children, one of the curses of widowhood.

"Would it help if I talked to her?"

"I don't know."

"You can't just do nothing."

"I know that much." Her voice was sharper than she intended. But she truly didn't know what to do and hated the helpless feeling.

Cooper said no more, which made her feel worse.

She'd spent the entire weekend trying to figure out the best route to take and had come up empty. Grounding didn't seem to do any good. Somehow she had to get to the root of Rose's objections.

"How's the scampi?" Cooper asked.

"The most luscious thing I've tasted in a long time."

His gaze dropped to her lips. "I can think of others."

She pointed at him and laughed. "Stop that."

"Why?"

"Because."

"Because it makes you want to kiss me?"

"Yes."

At the easy admission, he laughed. "Are we on for skating at Frog Pond tomorrow night? I know lots of kissing places there."

"You're a bad boy."

"Never said I wasn't."

"What time? Seven?" He'd promised the girls days ago to take them ice skating. Natalie loved to skate but hadn't been in ages. The idea of skating with Cooper, hand in his, was a temptation too strong to resist. If they happened to sneak a few kisses along the way, she wouldn't complain one bit.

The scent of wood smoke filled the crisp air as Cooper crossed Boston Common with Natalie and the twins at his side. Bundled in snowsuits, scarves and hats, their boots crunched on the new fallen snow.

The four of them held hands, a wide line of frosted laughter and anticipation. A warm, family feeling shifted past Cooper like a ghostly presence. What would it be like if this were his family? If these were his daughters? If Natalie were his wife?

He'd been having these thoughts too often lately. He knew better. He was no more in the market for a spouse than she was, but still the thoughts persisted.

Sometimes late at night, when he was home alone and the stresses of the day had been shared with Natalie either in person or by telephone, he considered his motivations. Was he thinking family thoughts because he cared for Natalie and the girls? Or because, in some twisted kind of way, he had to win her away from Justin.

He hoped it wasn't the latter. But he also had the fierce need to hear her admit that she was his and his alone.

"I think I forgot how to skate," Rose said, eyeing the rentals with uncertainty. Cooper and Natalie owned skates, but the twins didn't. Yet.

With an inward smile, he added skates to their growing Christmas list. Natalie would have a fit, but she'd get over it. He couldn't wait to see their faces on Christmas morning. He liked Natalie's little girls, even Rose in all her orneriness touched a tender place inside him. He wanted her to approve of him, both for Natalie's sake and for his own.

"We'll help you get started again. In fact, we'll all hold hands and skate together for a while." After plunking down the required fees, he handed out skates, which they carried to one of the many benches.

A smattering of skaters circled the frozen pond while others watched from the lighted railing. Greenery and red bows decorated the front of the warming kiosk where, no doubt, the girls would require plenty of hot chocolate. Boston glowed bright and golden in the near distance, and the circle of trees around the pond wore the seasonal loops of glittering holiday lights. It was a great night for ice-skating and hanging out with the people who mattered.

Might as well admit it — Natalie, Lily and Rose mattered. He was still analyzing the reasons, but they definitely mattered.

As soon as they were laced up, Natalie stood and held out both hands. "Come on. Who's first?"

"All for one and one for all." Cooper took Lily's hand and helped her to her feet, handing her off to Natalie. Prepared for rejection, he offered Rose the same assistance. Amazingly, she slipped a gloved hand in his and stood on wobbly legs. He grinned down at her tense, jutting chin. In all her stubborn determination, she was the image of her mother. "Put the girls in between us until they get their skating legs under them."

According to Natalie, both girls could roller-skate and had ice-skated in the past, so he expected them to regain their confidence in no time.

"Do I have to wear this helmet?" Lily tugged a secure chin strap.

"Yes, you do. No cracked skulls this close to Christmas." Natalie playfully tapped her daughter on the pink headgear. "Come on, now. It's not too crowded tonight. We're going to have so much fun."

Side by side, the four of them started out by walking a few steps to get balanced and then began to glide slowly around the ice. Rose skated next to Cooper. Her gloved hand held his tightly, her body stiff with uncertainty.

"You're doing fine, princess. Relax. Bend your knees a little more. And just go with the flow."

She looked at him from the corner of her eye, her chin tilting up the slightest bit. She wouldn't give up. He knew that for sure. It was one of the things he admired the most about Rose. Whether playing board games or working out math problems, when she tilted that chin, she would succeed or die in the effort. He could relate.

Lily got the hang of skating much faster, which surprised Cooper. Rose was usually the athletic one.

"I want to skate faster, Mom," Lily said, shaking loose from Rose's other hand. The action almost tumbled her twin, but Cooper kept her upright.

"Rose isn't ready for speed yet."

Rose shook her head, expression tense, refusing to let go of Cooper's hand even for a second. He didn't know if it was his size advantage or skating expertise to which Rose clung, but by whatever miracle, she wanted to stay with him.

"You two go ahead," he offered. "Rose and I need to take things slow for a while."

"Are you sure?" Natalie glanced from Rose to Cooper and back again, her doubtful expression saying she fully expected them to do one another in. Cooper winked and tried not to laugh. He was having fun courting the pugnacious Rose. She'd thrown down the gauntlet and he'd accepted the challenge. Not that he wouldn't have liked to be skating with Natalie, too, but that would come. He'd see to it.

Eyes focused straight ahead, Rose lifted one hand in a dismissing shoo. "Go."

Natalie and Lily needed no more encouragement. With a jaunty wave, they glided away.

Faster skaters sailed past. Couples, arms

181

around waists and eyes only for each other, swished by. The *swoosh, swish* of blades cutting ice filled the crisp night air.

He and Rose skated on, slowly, steadily, with Rose's fingers so tense in his, he felt sorry for her. For the first time he wondered if Rose's brattiness stemmed from fear. Fear of the unknown, fear of change, fear of losing someone she loved. Again.

Could fear be the reason she objected to him? Because she was afraid of losing her mother? Of losing the good memories of her father?

It was something to think about.

After a few minutes, when she hadn't slipped or fallen, some of the stiffness eased from Rose's shoulders. She even dared to turn her head to one side long enough to find her mother and sister across the pond. They waved. Cooper returned the greeting.

A group of college men mistook Natalie's wave as meant for them and skated close to her. Her smile flashed and she said something.

Cooper suffered a foolish male reaction. Possessiveness.

Before he had sufficiently tucked away the feeling, Rose hit him with, "Mom has lots of boyfriends."

"Really?" He eyed the trio of males, chatting up his date. For a second, jealousy was a gut-eating tiger. Then he laughed. "Rose, I don't think that's true."

"Yes, it is. They kiss all the time."

Ah, now they were getting somewhere. "Does that upset you?"

The question stopped her for a minute. She gazed up at him, eyes troubled. "I don't know. It's kinda gross."

Cooper hid a smile. She was dead serious and talking. No point in infuriating her with the obvious. To him, kissing Natalie was anything but gross.

He was smart enough to know that Rose's objections had nothing to do with kissing and everything to do with Justin.

"Tell me about your dad," he said softly. "What's your best memory?"

She thought awhile, forehead wrinkled in concentration. "I liked it when he came home. He was gone a lot."

"You know why, don't you?"

"He was a doctor."

"Yes, and he helped a lot of people. But he worked hard for other reasons, too."

She relaxed enough to look up at him. "He did?"

"You." He tapped her pink nose with one finger. "And Lily and your mother. Your dad

183

worked hard so that you could have a good life."

"I miss him."

"Yeah, me, too." The words came from his heart and as such, carried the sadness he felt at the loss of a good man and maybe even a shade of guilt for wanting to take Justin's place. Rose responded to the emotion with a quizzical stare. "It's okay to miss your dad," he added. "but it's okay to be my friend, too."

After a second her gray eyes clouded. "Sometimes I can't remember. Mom has to show us the videos."

The admission squeezed his heart. At six she had barely been old enough to remember anything, but she must feel guilty, viewing her failed memory as an insult to her father.

"Mom's coming." She motioned across the way. At some point in their conversation, Rose's awkwardness had disappeared so that her small feet now glided easily over the ice. They may not have accomplished much as far as making friends, but at least she was more confident on the ice.

"She has someone with her."

Natalie, along with Lily and an older, distinguished-looking couple skated in their direction.

As they grew closer, Cooper recognized Natalie's boss, Belle Mackenzie. The friendly looking man was a stranger.

"Is this a setup?" Natalie whispered to Belle as the four of them swished closer to Cooper and Rose.

The moment Belle and Charlie had appeared on the ice, Natalie had been suspicious. Though she had to admit, her elegant, full-figured boss skated with eye-catching grace and dignity, her long red scarf flowing out behind. This wasn't her first visit to Frog Pond.

"Of course it's a setup, sugar," Belle said with a throaty chuckle. "How are you and Cooper ever going to be alone unless your friends interfere?" She patted her date's hand. "Charlie here was kind enough to accompany me. Wasn't that thoughtful?"

The besotted look Charlie gave her relayed far more than thoughtfulness. Natalie leaned close to Belle and whispered, "He has the hots for you."

"I heard that," Charlie said, friendly eyes crinkling. "And you are absolutely right."

"Oh, Charlie," Belle simpered in such an un-Belle like manner. Whether her boss admitted it or not, she and Charlie were falling in love. All the Belles would be happy

185

to see their friend and mentor happily wed to Serena's new father-in-law.

"Why aren't you still in Tahoe with the newlyweds?"

"Three's a crowd on a honeymoon, sweetie," Belle said. "Just as four can be a crowd on a romantiç skating date."

"This is not a —" By now they'd reached Cooper and Rose, so Natalie's protest died in her throat. Maybe Belle was right. Maybe it *was* a date, but no use getting Rose stirred up. From the looks of her daughter and Cooper, they'd survived the last few minutes without killing each other. Maybe there was hope, after all.

Ice spraying lightly, they skidded to a stop.

"Look who we found," she said. "Cooper, you know Belle, and this is Charles Wiley."

The men shook hands.

"Great night for skating," Cooper offered, his impeccable manners always impressive.

Belle fanned her face in the most atrociously fake Southern belle affectation Natalie had ever seen. "Yes, indeed, but we old-bones have to rest a bit. I am completely fatigued."

Yeah, right, and Natalie was Mary Poppins. Belle had the energy of three women half her age.

Cooper fell right into Belle's manoeuvering. "The kiosk is a great place to rest. We could all go for hot chocolate if you'd like."

"No, no. You and Natalie have hardly gotten started. But I'm thinking these two little chicks could use a rest and a snack."

"Us?" Rose asked hopefully, pointing from herself to Lily.

"None other. Come on," Belle said, eyes sparkling as she shooed the twins together like a mother hen. "Uncle Charlie and I have a surprise for you in the kiosk."

"Sugar cookies?" Rose asked, eyes alight.

"Hot chocolate with marshmallows?" Lily put in.

"Lots and lots of marshmallows," Belle said, giving Natalie one last look, eyebrow arched in humorous speculation, before skating away with the twins.

"That was nice of them," Cooper said, grinning from ear to ear.

"Did you ask her to do that?"

He laughed, the sexy sound shimmering through Natalie with the warmth of the hot chocolate her girls were so excited about.

"I would have if I'd thought of it." He held his hands out to each side. "Just you and me, babe. What do you say? Shall we explore the dark corners and shaded nooks?"

A thrill zipped through her blood. "I say you're crazy and so are my friends."

"I like your friends." Still grinning in that adorable, sexy way, he spun around to face her, skating backward with all the skill and athleticism of an Olympian.

"Show-off," she said, and then ducked past him and sped away, laughing at the shock on his face.

Though she could skate, her shorter legs were no match for Cooper's longer ones. In seconds he sailed by, did a fast figure eight, then skidded to a stop, spraying snow up into their faces.

Though she saw it coming, Natalie couldn't stop in time and plowed into him. Down they went in a tangle of arms and legs and laughter.

Somehow Cooper, agile and quick, landed on the bottom, strong hands breaking her fall. Nevertheless, she sprawled atop him, acutely aware of the rise and fall of his chest, of the hard maleness of his body. Longing curled and heated inside her like pine boughs on a campfire.

"You okay?" His concern was tinged with laughter.

"This ice is cold."

"Cold? From my vantage point, it's hard."

"Hard and cold," she corrected, feeling light and carefree and a little too happy.

Cooper's warm breath soughed against

her lips. She leaned down, touched her mouth to his. The combination of cold lips and warm mouth was a pleasant shock.

When she immediately pushed away and started to sit up, Cooper pulled her back down. "Wait a minute, lady. My turn. I'm the injured party here."

Holding her face in his gloved hands, he kissed her with such sweetness, such gentle emotion that her insides hummed a new and unfamiliar song. The curl of longing returned in full force.

Cooper Sullivan was messing with her mind.

And maybe her heart.

CHAPTER NINE

The days before Christmas passed in a whirlwind of baking for dozens of parties and weddings, shopping for Rose and Lily, wrapping gifts and thinking about Cooper. Yes, always Cooper. Though she refused to analyze the situation, she was not naive. Something was going on. She just didn't know what.

She'd even baked a French Christmas Cake, loaded with rum-flavored chocolate filling for Cooper's nursing staff, along with special cakes for all her friends and a dozen for the homeless shelter. By Christmas morning she was both weary and unreasonably happy.

Fresh out of the shower, she leaned into the bathroom mirror and grinned. Yep. That was a happy face.

After testing her blood sugar, she injected the required dose of insulin and put her supplies away. Glucose was up this morning, compliments of the sinfully delicious petit fours she'd devoured yesterday afternoon at the Belle's annual Christmas Eve party. She'd have to go easy today or pay the price.

She could almost hear Justin scolding her. She went into the bedroom and picked up his picture. It had been weeks since she'd talked to him this way.

"I'm a big girl now. I can handle it." He smiled back at her with a twinkling look that said he didn't believe a word.

This time, the tearing grief and fury didn't come. At long last she was healing, standing strong with no one to lean on but herself. She was proud of that.

She replaced the photo and went into the living room where the Christmas tree lights reflected off the bright and shiny packages below.

Even after she'd instructed Cooper not to go overboard on gifts, he'd dropped by last night with an armload of boxes. She'd threatened to throw him out. He'd only laughed and claimed they were repayment for the fancy cranberry cake she'd promised to bake for his family. The truth was she couldn't stay mad at Cooper. She tried, but he had a way about him that got to her every time.

In the quiet living room, Natalie cradled a cup of coffee and breathed in the smell of Christmas morning. Peppermint and pine. Cinnamon and sage.

"Merry Christmas, Mommy!" Lily and Rose charged in, breaking her moment of quiet reflection. She set aside her coffee in favor of hugs and kisses, though the twins were too excited to allow much of that. While Natalie's heart wanted to hold them and reminisce about every Christmas with her babies, Rose and Lily bounced around with the energy of live electric lines, unaware of how emotional the morning was for their mother.

"Can we open them now?"

No use trying to get them to eat breakfast first. At Christmas all the rules about proper diet went out of the window as soon as the stockings were opened.

"Go for it." She sat down on the couch, camera in hand to soak up the magical moments of childhood. She'd learned the hard way to treasure every second. Life was a fleeting thing.

Paper flew, children exclaimed and giggled while the radio played "Silent Night," "Rudolph" and myriad other Christmas carols.

Natalie was happy. Life was good.

The doorbell chimed and life got better.

Cooper, dressed in full Santa gear, stood at the door, ho-ho-hoing for all he was worth.

His disguise fooled exactly no one.

"Cooper!" Lily squealed and rushed his knees.

Rose, in the middle of ripping open a Barbie salon head, jumped up from the floor. "I knew it was you."

Laughing, Natalie motioned him inside. "I thought you were spending Christmas with your family in Cambridge."

Cooper patted his padded belly and went right on with the charade. "Santa doesn't live in Cambridge. He lives at the North Pole."

"Then where's Rudolph?" Rose asked eyeing the fake beard as if longing to give it a tug.

"Pulled up lame after a rough landing in Baltimore. I had to rent a truck."

"Must have been tough for Santa getting all those presents into an SUV," Natalie said.

"You don't know the half of it. But here they are." He reached behind him on the porch where a huge box of gifts waited.

"Cooper! I told you no more gifts."

"Cooper?" he said, patting his padded belly. "Who is this Cooper? Sounds like a terrific guy. I want to meet him."

"Oh, get in here before you let all the heat out of the house."

In moments, her usually subdued Christmas morning turned into a three-ring circus. Even Rose couldn't resist the fun of Cooper's high-energy version of a very silly Santa. He told stories, made up outlandish lies about reindeer and the North Pole, and handed out wrapped presents as though he really were the jolly old elf.

Watching him with the girls, his Santa beard sliding up and down every time he talked in a deep, ho-ho-ho voice that sent both girls into giggling fits, Natalie finally faced the facts.

She was falling in love with Cooper Sullivan. She didn't know whether to rejoice or subside into a deep depression. He was all the things she'd promised never to have in her life again. A bossy, overconfident, take-charge man who spent too much money and considered her helpless. Well, maybe not helpless exactly. Cooper seemed proud of her accomplishments. He thought she was a great mom and a terrific baker. She appreciated that.

But there were two major problems with falling for Cooper. First, Rose. Even though she was happy today, all kids were happy on

Christmas. At any minute the notorious Puppy could appear and destroy the idyllic scene.

More than that was the little problem of Cooper himself. Yes, he'd kissed her and held her and made his desire very clear. But he'd never mentioned love, never mentioned any wish to settle down with one woman, especially a woman with two children, one of whom could be a trifle troublesome. In fact, he'd made it clear that just the opposite was true. All his talk centered on a determination to be chief of cardiac surgery and the hours and dedication it took to gain that position. A family was light-years away.

"What about Mommy?" Lily asked from her perch on Cooper's knee. "Did you bring her a present?"

"Lily, that's not polite." He'd already given her an oven, for crying out loud.

"Santa doesn't care, do you Santa?" Lily asked.

"He's not Santa, dumb-wad," Rose said as she popped a chocolate reindeer into her mouth. From the telltale ring around her lips, this wasn't her first piece of candy.

"Rose," Natalie warned, praying that Rose wouldn't ruin the lovely morning with one of her moods. "Don't be rude to your sister, and save some of that candy for later."

Cooper gently set Lily on her feet. All the while, his twinkling gaze held Natalie captive. "Has your mommy been good?"

"I'm always good," Natalie answered. The words were perfectly innocent and neither child noticed anything, but the heat in Cooper's eyes gave *good* a whole new meaning.

"I don't doubt it a bit." When she slugged his red-sleeved arm, he pulled his beard down and laughed. "Padded."

She rolled her eyes. "Do you want some coffee? Or eggnog? Or anything at all to stuff in your big mouth?"

"Cookies," Lily chimed in. "Us and Mom made three kinds for you last night." She skipped into the kitchen and returned with a covered plate. Cooper chose one of each, popped them into his mouth and proclaimed them the best cookies ever.

"And Santa has eaten all kinds. Trust me on this."

Lily giggled, loving the charade, though she occasionally slipped up and called him Cooper. Rose remained watchful, but thankfully cooperative. Once in a while she'd forget her self-imposed reserve and interact with the pretend Santa.

Natalie breathed a sigh of relief that Cooper hadn't bought more gifts for her.

She'd thought about getting him something a half-dozen times, but in the end she and the girls had settled on a simple handcrafted gift from the three of them. What could she, a single mom with piles of debt, possibly buy for Cooper Sullivan?

"So," Cooper said after all the gifts were unwrapped, and shiny paper and bows littered the living room. "Would the three of you like to go to Cambridge with me after dinner?"

Natalie peeked in the oven at the turkey and then at Cooper. "To your place?"

"To my father and mother's house."

His serious look gave her pause, but after checking the yams, she answered, "If you're sure you want to take two over-stimulated eight-year-olds."

"Nothing would make me happier."

Nothing? Natalie experienced a flutter of nerves at the idea of meeting his family. Wasn't that supposed to mean something?

Late that afternoon, after too much of Natalie's turkey and oyster stuffing and coconut cream pie, Cooper dreaded the expected visit to his family home. Having long since discarded the Santa suit in favor of slacks and pullover sweater, he helped Natalie bundle the twins into coats and hats for the short drive to Cambridge.

Natalie had spit-shined the girls into fancy red Christmas dresses and black patent shoes, pulling each one's blond hair up on the sides into bunches. The pair looked like a television commercial. Natalie had disappeared into the back of the house only to return in a simple black skirt and blue sweater that drew attention to her beautiful eyes. Her hair was down for once, straight and smooth and soft around her face. She took his breath away, and he loved looking at her.

He was grateful to her too. His mother would have laid on the guilt for months if he'd skipped Christmas. Having Natalie and the girls along should ease the tension.

By the time they'd reached the elegant mansion where Cooper had grown up, his overstuffed stomach was in knots.

"You don't look too happy," Natalie remarked as they exited the car.

What could he say? That he dreaded time spent with his own family because they were disappointed in him?

He gave her a noncommittal smile and pressed the doorbell. His mother, in pearls and an understated designer dress opened the door at once.

"Cooper, darling. We'd almost given you

up." His mother's words were a gentle rebuke. He'd let the family down by not arriving earlier.

"Merry Christmas, Mother." He kissed her cheek.

Inside the foyer, bedecked with swags and garlands, they were joined by his father. Cooper made the introductions. Natalie, smile warm, handed over the baker's box. "I made this especially for you."

"How very thoughtful." His mother lifted the lid. "Oh my. This is fabulous. You're very good."

"Thank you. It was Cooper's idea, actually. He wanted you to have something special for the holidays."

His mother beamed and showed them into the vast living room. Score one for Natalie.

His brother, Cameron, and his pregnant wife, Darla, were ensconced in front of the crackling fireplace sipping wassail. Conversation at first was stiff as it always was when he gathered with his family. They chatted a bit about Cam's run for office, talking strategy as the family had done for as long as he could remember. Life in the Sullivan household ebbed and flowed around elections.

Finally his father turned toward him. "So how are things going with you, Cooper?"

"Fine." What the congressman really wanted to know was when he would make Chief. He was working on it.

"No chance you've changed your mind about public service?"

His dad always had to turn the screw, to make him feel as if he was cheating society by not running for office. "Sorry. I belong in a hospital, not the state house."

"Cooper replaced two valves in an infant this week," Natalie said, her voice proud. "And the baby is doing well."

"Really? How nice." His father had no clue how rare such a procedure was. "I trust they paid you well for that. We'll expect a donation to Cam's campaign."

The congressman's laugh boomed but Cooper saw no humor. His work wasn't about the money, though he made plenty. It was about the expression on the parents' faces when he told them their baby had a fighting chance. He didn't expect his father to ever understand that or the hours of planning and study he'd spent before taking the child into the OR.

"Why don't we try some of this wonderful cake?" his mother said, clearly bored with the topic.

With an inward sigh, Cooper resigned himself to an afternoon of stiff conversation and awkward explanations. All the while, he wished to be back in Natalie's tiny house. Here, approval was contingent on success. At Natalie's all he needed was himself and, he thought with a smile, a rented Santa suit.

"You're quiet," Natalie said on the way home.

"Don't want to wake the sleeping princesses." He cast a lopsided grin at her.

"What's the deal with you and your parents? They're nice."

"You can't tell me you were comfortable back there."

"Only because I don't know them well, and I worried one of the twins or I would embarrass you."

"You could never do that." In fact, she was the buffer that had made those few hours almost pleasant.

"You didn't answer my question. Why so tense with your family? You weren't yourself at all."

"I have no right to complain. I'm fortunate to be their son."

"But?" She turned in the seat, raising one knee so that her bare leg almost touched his thigh. He nearly forgot the question. He was dying to kiss her. Had been all day, but with the twins ever-present, he hadn't wanted to start trouble on Christmas Day.

Hands gripping the steering wheel, he focused on the glare of on-coming lights. "Let's just say they — meaning my father — planned for me to join him in the law firm with an eye to politics."

"That's not unusual is it, for a dad to want his son to follow in his footsteps?"

"Cameron did. Dad was ecstatic when he graduated Harvard. Only Harvard would do for a Sullivan."

"And you attended UMass. Any reason why?"

"Because you were there?"

"Ha. You didn't even know me then."

"Rebellion, maybe. I wasn't interested in law. I wanted to fix people. Dad was not pleased."

"Your parents didn't want you to become a physician?" she asked, expression incredulous in the glow of dash lights.

"They never actually said as much, but the expectation was there. Attending UMass instead of Dad's alma mater was a sacrilege."

"They're proud of you. Anyone can see that. They just have a different way of expressing their pride."

"You think I'm being childish?"

"Yes. Get over yourself, Doc."

He gave a short laugh. Maybe she was right. Even if she weren't, he couldn't change his parents, but he could change his attitude. "See? That's why you're good for me."

Eyes on the road, he felt in the darkness for her hand. Making contact with the smooth skin of her knee first, he thought about exploring that particularly pleasant area for a while. But the girls were in the back seat. Soon he had to get Natalie alone.

He found her hand and tugged. She scooted closer, bringing with her the scent of light cologne.

"What are you doing on New Year's Eve?" he asked.

"Hmm. I usually stay home and ring in the New Year in my pajamas, but Regina and Dell are hosting a big party."

"Are you going?"

Her gaze flickered up to his. "I don't know. Regina said I could bring a date."

A smile bloomed in his chest. "Are you asking?"

Her smile flashed in the dim light. "She did happen to mention your name."

"See? I told you I like your friends." He pulled down the signal lever and made a left turn. "Do you mind if we stop by my place for a few minutes?"

She glanced at the dash clock. "It's still early. Sure. Why not?"

He hitched his chin toward the back seat. "What about the sleeping beauties?"

"Trust me, they are not down for the night. This is a cat nap, so they can keep going and going."

"Great." He relaxed a little. Natalie's Christmas gift awaited, but he needed the right moment to give it to her.

In ten minutes they entered the posh town house. The cleaning woman had been in the day before and the fresh scent of potpourri filled the air.

"This is a beautiful place, Cooper."

The twins stood in the center of the room, shaking off the remnants of their nap. Rose, coming to life first, looked around with a frown. "Where's your Christmas tree?"

"At your house."

Lily pursed her mouth in concern. "That's sad."

"It is, isn't it?" And Cooper saw that it truly was, though he had never put up a tree in the years since leaving home. He liked Christmas, but a tree seemed like a lot of trouble for a man alone with no one to share the pleasure. "There's a game room through there. You're welcome to check it out."

The twins exchanged looks and then were off, disappearing into the room where they'd find enough to keep them busy for a week.

"Could I offer you a drink? Some wine?"

"That would be nice. Yes. I've. been pretty good today. Maybe it won't drive my blood sugar crazy."

He poured the wine, handed her a slender glass and lifted his in toast. "Merry Christmas."

She clinked his glass. "Merry Christmas."

Feeling a little more jittery than he'd expected, he went to the side bar for the velvet bag waiting there. "I bought you a gift."

She shook her head but her dimples betrayed her. "I told you no more."

His mouth tipped up as he handed her the bag. Oh man, he wanted to kiss her. "Don't spoil my Christmas."

She slid the long, jewelers' box from the drawstring bag. Cooper held his breath as she opened the lid.

"Oh, my." She traced the necklace with the tips of her fingers. "Cooper."

"I want to see it on you." He lifted the curved diamond pendant from the box. With a question in her eyes, Natalie turned her back so he could drape the chain around

205

her neck. When she lifted her hair the scent of spice and shampoo filled his nostrils. He breathed in, holding the sweet scent, cherishing the moment. The clasp closed, he placed a kiss on her neck just below the hairline. Natalie shivered, and he kissed her there again. "Like it?"

"I love it."

He turned her toward him. Her hands rested on the curved diamond. Her blue, blue eyes swam with emotion. "You shouldn't have."

"I wanted to make you happy."

She didn't respond with words. Instead, she walked into his arms and kissed him. His heart soared as surely as his blood raced. She hadn't fought him over the diamonds. Maybe now was the right timing for the idea he'd been tossing around.

"I've been thinking about something, Natalie," he said, holding her face in his hands so he could kiss her in between thoughts. "Something that makes perfect sense to me." He kissed her nose, and she sighed. "I'd like you and the girls to move in with me."

Natalie jerked. "What?"

He held her still, kissed her nose again, though the tension in her body said she wanted to pull away. "Think about it. We're attracted to each other. We're good company. And you wouldn't have the expense of maintaining a household."

She'd be here where he could provide for her and the girls, could see they were safe, could protect them, and if he and Natalie shared a room, that would be all the better.

She blinked at him as though the words weren't soaking in. "You're asking me to move in with you?"

"There's plenty of room, a clubhouse, lots of amenities." He was sounding like a real estate salesman. "I think it would be best."

"You think it would be best," she repeated slowly. "Best for whom?"

"Well, you and the girls, of course."

"What about you? What do you get out of it?"

You. But he didn't say that. He knew without a doubt, she would not appreciate that comment. "Someone to talk to when I'm here."

"And someone to sleep with?"

"That's up to you."

"Is it?"

"You know my work schedule, the research and study I do. I'm gone a lot." He'd already told her about the upcoming trip to the conference in Zurich.

"So I'll live here in your fancy town house

alone with my girls while you're off pursuing the brass ring? And once in a while, you'll come home for some cozy time and a laugh or two and be gone again?"

Her voice was calm and quiet, but he had a bad feeling she did not like his suggestion.

"That's not what I meant."

"Isn't it? I know your type, Cooper. You're too success driven to settle down."

How could he deny what was true?

"In a few years, I'll be chief of surgery and then —"

"And then you'll be shooting for chief of staff."

He couldn't deny it. Medicine was his life. It was what he wanted, what he needed. Wasn't it? "Is that wrong?"

She shook her head sadly. "No. Of course not. You'll become the best chief they've ever had."

The words should have been a compliment but Cooper suspected he'd failed her somehow.

"That's my dream. What about you? Don't you want something more out of life than baking cakes?"

She tilted her head in thought. Her hand went to the diamond at her throat. He loved seeing it there.

Her shoulders twitched in a slight shrug.

"Nothing quite so lofty and grand as your ambitions, I fear. I want my business to do well. Believe it or not, I like baking cakes. I want a quiet life with my family. And maybe someday I'll have a big old rambling house with a backyard for the kids to play in. Simple things."

Simple things. He couldn't even begin to imagine. And yet, her dream sounded so much warmer, so much more fulfilling than his.

Why was that, he wondered.

CHAPTER TEN

Natalie was as nervous as a teenager on prom night. She hadn't been out on New Year's Eve since — well, in a long time. After spending two days and fifty dollars online, she'd found an evening dress befitting the date of an up-and-coming young surgeon whose status as the handsome, charming, and eligible son of a U.S. Representative often landed his photos in the society column.

Sitting in front of her vanity mirror, she attached a pair of dangly diamond earrings, borrowed from Regina, to go with the necklace Cooper had given her.

She paused, touched the diamond sparkling against her throat. He'd hurt her feelings that night and yet the poor man hadn't a clue why. She could see it in his baffled expression. Even after all the times she'd told him she could stand on her own two feet, he truly did not understand why she would not move in with him.

Adorable, exasperating man.

She still grappled to understand why he'd offered in the first place. Did he still feel some misguided obligation? Or was he trying to win her over now because he'd never been able to do so when Justin was alive? Or was there a chance that he, too, felt this magical thing growing between them?

Since Christmas, neither had mentioned that moment of tension at his town house, and she didn't plan to bring it up again. Still, she wondered. Why was Cooper seeing so much of her when he had no desire to settle down?

She shook away the thought. Whatever the reason, she wanted to be with him. She was falling in love with him, and even if their relationship went no further than tonight, she would not regret the time they'd had together. As she well knew from her marriage to Justin, no matter how long it lasted, love was a beautiful experience worth the risk.

Her mind centered on the thought. When had she changed her mind? When had she stopped worrying so much about losing her independence in exchange for time in Cooper's company? When had she begun to hope again?

"Mommy." Rose came in the room and leaned against her back.

Natalie glanced at her daughter's mirrored reflection. "Hey, punkie. Shannon should be here any minute. She's bringing pizza." Shannon was the best teenage babysitter money could buy. The girls loved her bag of tricks, games and activities.

"My tummy hurts."

Natalie spun around on the vanity chair to place a hand on Rose's forehead. "No fever. Maybe you're just hungry."

Rose shook her head. "No. I'm sick, Mom. I don't think you should leave me here with a babysitter. She might not know what to do with a sick kid."

Ah. So that was it. "Cooper will be here soon." She kissed her daughter's forehead. "We'll ask him to make sure you're okay before we leave."

Looking none too happy, Rose dragged along behind Natalie into the living room and collapsed dramatically onto the couch. "I might have something contagious. Shannon could get sick."

The doorbell rang and Cooper came inside. Natalie's mouth watered. In a black tux, he was about the most delicious-looking man she'd ever seen. She literally wanted to eat him up.

"Wow," Cooper said. "You look fabulous."

If he'd noticed her glazed, infatuated stare, he said nothing. "Thank you. You do, too."

Her glitzy teal dress fit her like a glove and struck just above her knee. The back was cut low and made her feel sexy and feminine.

"Cooper!" Lily came flying down the hallway and threw herself against the good doctor's legs. Without thought to his elegant attire, he swooped her high into the air, making her laugh with glee. When he'd set her down again, he took two party blowers from his pocket.

"To ring in the New Year," he said and was rewarded with Lily's cute-as-pie smile.

"I've got a loose tooth," she said, showing him.

As if fascinated, he crouched to peer at the wiggly incisor. "What's the Tooth Fairy paying these days?"

While Cooper and Lily chit-chatted about teeth and the Tooth Fairy, pleasure rose inside Natalie as warm as a June day. Cooper was good for her and good for her kids.

Rose began to sniffle. "I'm sick, Mommy. Don't go."

Well, at least one of her kids.

213

"I was going to ask you to have a look at her before we leave," Natalie told Cooper. "She says her stomach hurts, but she's not been sick all day. No fever. I'm thinking . . ." She let the thought trail away.

Cooper nodded in understanding and settled onto the edge of the sofa beside her daughter. "Tell me where it hurts, Rose."

Her daughter went into a litany of complaints that had both Cooper and Natalie fighting grins. After a bit, Cooper said, "You have a bad case of malingering."

Rose seemed delighted. She popped up and stared at Natalie. "I told you I was sick."

"Do you think she needs medication, Doctor?" Natalie asked. "And straight to bed with no television or pizza?"

"Hmm. Possibly."

"And no games with Shannon or Lily?"

"Rose's worried gray eyes moved from her mother to Cooper and back again. "You're going even though I am sick, aren't you?"

Natalie suffered a twinge of guilt. What if Rose really was ill? Cooper must have seen her wavering because he said, "She'll be fine, Natalie."

"Yes, of course she will." She didn't understand why she felt so guilty. Rose was notorious for these kinds of shenanigans. The aches and pains and complaints of

214

recent weeks had all been concocted to separate Natalie and Cooper. Rose would be fine. "Shannon has my cell number."

"I'll leave mine, too."

As soon as Shannon arrived and was apprised of the situation, Natalie and Cooper departed, though Rose's betrayed glare followed her mother all the way to the party.

Cooper watched Natalie fidget with the silver chain on her minuscule purse. Live music from the local band kicked into a rocky rhythm. The ballroom was comfortably crowded with stylish guests having a great time. Though the party was in full swing and tuxedoed waiters sashayed amidst the revelers offering canapés and wine, Natalie had yet to completely relax and enjoy the celebration. She'd chatted and smiled and said all the right things, but he could tell her mind was on Rose.

"Want to call her again?" he asked.

"What?" Her gaze flickered to his. "No, no. Of course not."

"Then why so distracted? Is your sugar acting up?"

"No. But I can't shake the feeling that I'm missing something where Rose is concerned. That there is more to Rose's mischief than a child vying for attention."

"What do you think it could be?"

Her shoulders relaxed as she emitted a self-deprecating laugh. "I have no idea. Mother's angst, I suppose."

Rose was accomplishing exactly what she'd set out to do — ruin their date. It irked him that Natalie let her get away with it. He tried to be understanding, but come on. A child should not run her mother's life.

Rose didn't seem to mind when Cooper was at the house. In fact, since the night at Frog Pond she no longer told the invisible dog to bite him and even joined in the play with him and Lily. Her misbehavior occurred whenever Cooper and Natalie wanted to be alone. Which would happen a lot more often if he had his way.

Natalie shook her head. Wisps of pale hair floated prettily around her face and grazed the soft pink of her luscious lips. His date looked stunning tonight. He'd told her as much. With her hair swept up except for those enchanting tendrils, diamonds dancing from her earlobes, her petite body encased in an elegant dress with enough sex appeal to make him whimper, he couldn't wait to get her into his arms.

He thought about that a lot lately. Holding her. Hearing her laugh. Making her happy. He was still trying to make up for upsetting her at Christmas, even though she seemed to have forgiven him. Too bad she hadn't agreed to move into the town house. He was convinced doing so would solve several problems at once, but he was not about to mention the subject again. There were always other ways to take care of her.

He'd been giving the topic a great deal of thought. Maybe his motives were screwed up, but he felt something powerful for the woman across from him.

When she fretted, like now, he nearly went crazy with wanting to make her world right. To his way of thinking that was a man's job. That's what a man did when he cared for a woman.

There was the crux of the issue. He cared for Natalie, a lot. At first she'd been a prize to win. Now she was a treasure to hold. He didn't want her hurt or upset. He just plain wanted her.

He went crazy thinking that she might still be in love with Justin. And crazier still because he wasn't sure he could ever be the kind of man that made her happy.

If he had any sense at all, he needed to keep his mind on his career and off Natalie. He should, but he couldn't.

"Would you rather skip the dancing and

auction, head back to your house early?" he asked.

"Absolutely not. We can't let her do this to us."

A smile bloomed in his chest. "My thoughts exactly. No more worries, only fun tonight. Agreed?"

"Agreed." She smiled, the flashing dimples and bow mouth creating fantasies in his mind.

Just then, their hostess, Regina, shuffled through the crowd. In sparkling red heels, the dark-haired beauty towered over Natalie. She placed both hands on her hips. "Why aren't you two dancing? Aren't you having fun?"

"Great party, Regina," Cooper said smoothly. Natalie had told him that the Belles' photographer was sometimes self-conscious about her husband's wealth and was still adjusting to being a rich woman.

"Have you bid on any of the silent auction items? All the money's going to a children's charity."

"Cooper has." The look Natalie gave him made his chest swell with pride. If she'd keep looking at him that way, he'd buy everything in the place.

"Don't look now, Regina," Natalie said, "but there is a very handsome man coming

218

your way with a decided gleam in his eye."

Regina's dark eyes lit up as her husband approached. "Oooh, goody. Doesn't he look scrumptious? Gotta go, kids." She took them both by the upper arm and shoved. "Now get out there and dance before I think you're not enjoying my party."

Cooper laughed and swept his date onto the floor. Natalie came, a small, but perfect fit against his body. Lithe and easy, she danced like a dream.

For the next hour, no more was said about the problem of Rose. They danced and laughed, talking about everything under the sun. That was one of the great things about Natalie. No matter how often they talked, there was always more to tell her. She listened as though his work, his life, his golf game were the most important matters on her mind. Natalie had the knack of making a man feel like a man.

An hour before midnight and the fireworks display that promised to wow them all into the New Year, Natalie's cell phone jangled. She exchanged a quick look of dismay with him before answering.

After a terse conversation that did not bode well for his carefully planned evening, Natalie pushed the off button and sighed. "I'm sorry. We have to go."

"What's wrong?"

"The bathroom is flooded. Someone left the faucet on."

And he knew exactly who.

By the time Natalie and Cooper arrived home, Rose was sound asleep in her bed, but there was no denying who was responsible for the flooded bathroom and hallway.

"I'm sorry, Natalie," Shannon said, her young face flushed with embarrassment. "I didn't know the girls had left the water on in the tub. I guess I should have checked, but when Rose offered to clean up after her bath, I thought everything was okay."

"You didn't hear the water running?" Cooper asked, his dark gaze taking in the mess.

The blush deepened. "I guess we had the music on pretty loud. We were playing dance club."

One of the twins' favorite pastimes was dressing up in various outfits and choreographing their own dances. They loved to dance as much as she did. The louder the music, the better. She could totally relate. When she had the money again, she planned to put them both in lessons.

"I'm not upset with you, Shannon. Rose, on the other hand, is in big trouble."

"I don't think she meant to do it."

"Unfortunately, I think you're wrong. She knew exactly what it would take to get us home."

"I'll stay and help you clean up."

"That's not necessary." Cooper surprised them both by saying. "Natalie and I will do it. There's only room for one or two in that bathroom anyway."

"I'm really sorry."

Cooper reached for his wallet but Natalie stopped him with a furious look. No way was he paying her babysitter, especially after her child had ruined his evening. She gave Shannon the required sum and walked her to the door, assuring the sitter over and over again that she was not to blame.

Once Shannon was safely in her car Natalie said, "Rose is not going to talk her way out of punishment this time."

Cooper leaned against the kitchen counter, expression serious. "I hope you mean that."

For a nanosecond, Natalie stiffened but quickly forced the tension from her expression. Sometimes she *did* let Rose get away with too much.

"You're right. I know that." She offered him a diet soda from the fridge. When he shook his head, she stuck the can back inside and closed the door. "It's just so hard, Cooper. She's my baby and she's been through a lot."

"So have you. So has Lily. But you're dealing with it."

"Even when Rose was tiny, she was so stubborn."

"Nothing wrong with a strong will when it's channeled in the right direction."

"Well, stopping up the bathtub to ruin her mother's New Year's Eve date is not the right direction."

Cooper glanced at his watch. "Half hour until the ball drops in New York. We still have plenty of time to stanch the flood and maybe still do a little celebrating."

"You don't have to stay. I can take care of this myself."

"What? And ruin my lascivious New Year's Eve plans?"

"You can't get too lascivious in a flood."

"Ha. Watch me." He grinned that million-dollar grin, slid out of his jacket and began rolling up his sleeves.

There was something about a man in dress clothes, with sleeves rolled back on sinewy arms, the shirt opened at the neck that turned her on. Oh, heck, everything about Cooper turned her on. A delicious tingle raced down her spine.

She kicked off her heels and grabbed clean-up supplies. "I've never mopped in formal attire."

"First time for everything. Hand me a bucket."

"Are you sure about this?"

Her question came too late, he was already swabbing the decks like a pro, sopping up water, then wringing the sponge into the bucket. "See? No problem. I pretend it's blood."

"Cooper!"

He laughed at her aghast expression. "Sorry. Bad doctor's joke."

Justin had said things like that all the time. Black humor was a coping mechanism for physicians.

They worked companionably, he in a tux and she in the satiny teal dress. Each time they bumped, he tilted his head and kissed her nose. Or her hair. Or her shoulder. The latter gave her delicious shivers. If he was trying to seduce her, he was succeeding.

She was on her knees dabbing at a corner when drops of water splattered her bare back.

"Hey!" She spun around. "Watch it there, mister."

From his spot in the doorway, he flicked another bit at her. Mischief, far more dangerous than Rose's, danced across his face. "Come over here and make me."

She plopped the sponge into the sink and rose. "That's a challenge I can't ignore."

"I love a woman who rises to a challenge."

His figure of speech set her blood humming and her mind racing. She and Cooper were teetering on the verge of something that might be foolish or maybe even dangerous. But in spite of her hard-won independence, she was going where the moment led.

Hands wet, she marched across the room, careful not to slip and fall. Before she could deliver the intended sprinkles, Cooper's arms encircled her, yanking her down against him.

"Oh, too bad," he murmured, not a bit sorry. "You lost."

But when his mouth found hers, she didn't feel like a loser. Not in the least.

After the luscious sensation ended, Cooper murmured against her mouth, "You kiss pretty good for a cleaning lady."

"You kiss pretty good for a guy who smells like my daughter's bubble bath."

He made a face, then laughed and hugged her closer.

"What do you say we turn on the TV, open the bottle of champagne I commandeered from Regina and watch the ball drop?"

"Sounds like a deal to me. But you have to let me up first."

"Darn. I like having you under my control." He released her, helping her to her feet.

"Huh. That'll be the day."

When her foot slipped the tiniest bit, he reached for her elbow and steadied her.

"Don't fall. Or we'll have to play doctor." He pumped his eyebrows in a very wicked manner.

Natalie made a rude noise in the back of her throat and carefully picked her way to the sink. Even though she laughed him off, the idea of playing doctor with Cooper sent a flame of desire racing through her veins.

As she washed and dried her hands, Cooper intentionally bumped up against her in the tiny bathroom.

"Bully," she said and nudged him with her hip. His bigger body didn't budge. He chuckled.

What would it be like to have him here when she woke up in the mornings? To jockey for position at the sink next to his clean-smelling body. To watch him shave?

He slipped his arms around her from behind. Her surprised gaze flickered up to his in the mirror.

"We look good together," he murmured,

snuggling close so that his body was pressed full length against hers. "You and me."

She swallowed hard, suddenly at a loss for quips. They did look good. His dark head against her pale one. His intensely brilliant eyes next to her wide blue ones. He was warm and hard and strong, every inch of him wonderfully, powerfully male. The scent of him, spicy and clean, filled her nostrils.

He dropped a kiss on the side of her neck and her eyes fluttered closed. The sensation was so delicious. His warm breath puffed softly against her ear. She tilted her head, hoping he'd kiss her there. He didn't disappoint her.

She gripped the countertop and shivered.

"You like that?" The soft rumble of his voice vibrated against her ear. His tongue darted out, stroked her earlobe.

"Mmm, yes." Her voice was a breathy whisper.

"Open your eyes. I want you to see us. To see me." Something rough and wild tinged his intense whisper. "Look at me, Natalie."

She obeyed, captivated by the sensations running through her like liquid fire. What she saw made her knees tremble. Her eyelids drooped with passion. The flush of desire tinged her cheeks. But it was Cooper's expression that made her weak.

Gone was the urbane surgeon who charmed the world with a quip and his brilliant mind. He was a warrior king claiming his prize, marking his possession. His dark eyes glittered, holding her with such intensity she couldn't look away.

Slowly he stroked her arms, his gaze never leaving hers. When his fingers slid across her shoulders in a featherlight touch, traced her collarbones, found the hollow of her throat, her chest rose and fell as if she'd been running.

He was seducing her. No doubt about it.

When her eyelids threatened to flutter closed again, he stopped. "Don't close your eyes, Natalie. Look at me. Think of me tonight, no one else."

She had no idea what he meant by the fiercely whispered words, but her knees were trembling now with such ferocity she felt as if her bones were water. Watching his hands touch her, stroke her and seeing her own reaction to that magic was the most amazingly sensual thing she'd ever experienced.

"I think I may collapse," she whispered.

His nostrils flared. "I'll be there to catch you."

Would he? Would he always be here to catch her? She knew the terrible answer to that. "Always" was a promise no one could make.

Slowly he turned her around, never letting go for even a second. She felt safe, secure, even as he went on holding her gaze with his in that fierce possessive way.

"I've never felt so turned on in my life," she murmured.

A tiny smile lifted the corners of his mouth. "What else do you feel?"

"Beautiful. Sexy."

"You are."

"So are you." She caressed the side of his face, loving the faint roughness of whiskers against her soft skin.

He captured her fingers and kissed them one by one. "You know what else?"

His voice remained hushed, almost reverent. The idea that he was as moved as she shook her to the core. Something beautiful was going on here. And it both thrilled and scared her.

Was she ready for this?

The answer came in a rush of emotion. Though his take-control personality frightened her to pieces, she was completely in love with Cooper Sullivan.

"What?" she whispered, hoping he felt the same, but too scared to ask.

"I think something serious is happening here."

"Me, too."

"What are we going to do about it?"

"What do you have in mind?"

"I think you know."

Yes, she knew because she wanted him, too. She also wanted to do what was best and right for her children — and herself. "I want you, too, but not here and not now." How did she tell him? "I'm not the kind of woman who has affairs."

Surely he understood that after she'd refused to move in with him.

He leaned his forehead against hers and sighed. "I knew you'd say that."

Her heart beat erratically. Either she'd lose him for good or their relationship was about to take a giant step forward. "I care about you, Cooper." Boy, was that an understatement.

He tinkered with a tendril of her loosened hair. "Then be with me. You know I'll take care of you."

"Scary proposition," she whispered.

"Love always is."

Her pulse slammed into high gear. Was he saying that he'd changed his mind? That he could love her, too? That he could back away from his career enough to be the man she needed?

Life was taking an unexpected turn, both wonderful and terrifying, and Natalie could no more resist what was coming than she could sprout wings and fly.

"Well, don't you look like the cat who ate the cream," Belle said as soon Natalie walked into the shop two days later.

"I think the good doctor must have given her his own special brand of medicine," Audra said with a grin as she swung away from her computer. "Nothing like a love potion to put that dreamy look on a woman's face."

Julie widened her eyes in humorous speculation. "We saw the two of you sneak away from the party."

"We didn't sneak. Here, taste these." Natalie offered around a plate of cake samples she'd made especially for Julie. "Rose flooded the bathroom and forced us to leave early."

"Natalie, that's terrible." Belle's expression was one of concern and bewilderment.

Terrible wasn't the word for it. On New Year's day, after grounding Rose for the rest of the holidays, Natalie had had a long talk with her daughters. She and the girls had been sprawled together in Natalie's bed.

"We'll always love Daddy," she'd begun

after snuggling both girls close. "He'll always be right here in our hearts forever. But Daddy wouldn't want us to be alone and sad the way we've been for the last two years. He'd want someone to take good care of us like he did."

The last words had nearly choked her. She was shaky about relinquishing her hard-won independence, but this was language children could understand.

Rose's pert face clouded. "Are you and Cooper getting married?"

Natalie kissed her pouty mouth. "Right now we want to be together and see where things go. Cooper is a good man, Rosie-posy. He likes us. He likes you and me and Lily. This is a good thing. So please don't be sad or upset anymore. Will you try? Please. For Mommy?"

After a long moment of silence, Rose, expression grave, nodded. Natalie released the breath she'd been holding.

Maybe things would be better now.

And in fact they were. For a while. The next few days were a whirlwind of fun and falling in love again. Oh, neither said the words, but the emotion was there, and if Cooper was still a little wary of taking the complete plunge, she tried to be patient.

Though their individual careers kept them busy, Cooper and Natalie spent every spare moment together. Sometimes they took the twins sledding or to a movie. Sometimes they hired a sitter so she and Cooper could have an evening alone. Most of the time they just hung out, talking, kissing. Natalie felt as giddy and happy and carefree as a teenager. For the first time in so long, she felt as if she didn't have to carry the load alone. The knowledge was both scary and liberating.

What had made her think she could ever live her entire life without love?

On the day they built a snow doctor in the front yard, complete with stethoscope and blue surgical hat, life seemed just about perfect. Cooper was headed to Zurich tomorrow to present a paper at a prestigious conference and had taken the entire day off to spend with her and the twins.

"It's important, Nat," he'd told her about the trip, eyes shining with excitement. "A real feather in the cap to be invited."

She'd expected to feel resentment that his career was already stealing him away, but instead she'd been happy for him. She'd miss him like crazy, but it was only for a few days.

"That's because you are a brilliant surgeon

who is changing the world for the better."

"There is that," he'd said, laughing, when she bopped him on the arm.

So now, here they were in the small front yard of her duplex building a snow doctor.

"Mom, take our picture." Rose had confiscated Cooper's muffler and now wore it wrapped around her head like a turban. She struck a silly pose beside the snow doctor. Lily giggled and imitated her sister.

"Hey, who stole my scarf?" Cooper roared in mock anger as he charged toward Rose. She squealed and took off, circling the snowman with Cooper and Lily right behind. The joyful sounds filled Natalie with incredible hope.

As she pressed the camera shutter, capturing the magical moments, she began to believe that everything would work out. The scene before her looked like a wintry greeting card. Two little girls with rosy cheeks. A handsome man frolicking in the white wonderland.

A shower of snow struck her on the shoulder, dislodging the camera.

"You messed up my shot," she said, teasing.

The twins giggled and fired another volley. "It was Cooper's idea."

"Oh, it was, was it?" She spun toward the

perpetrator, a hand to her hip.

"Guilty as charged." Cooper swiped the camera and moved very close to her face, snapping away. "I wanted your attention."

She laughed, self-conscious, and backed away. "Stop. My nose is red."

"Your nose, like the rest of you, is beautiful."

"Why, Dr. Sullivan," she said in her best Scarlett O'Hara. "I didn't know you cared."

He dropped the camera in his pocket and stalked toward her, eyes twinkling. "Why don't I show you how much?"

The question made her pulse jump. Backing away, she held up a finger to stop his advance. He laughed and kept coming.

With a squeal, she spun and took off in a run, lumbering through the thick, powdery snow. In three seconds flat, Cooper had tackled her from behind, and they both went down like colliding linebackers.

Natalie was laughing so hard, she could hardly breathe. Snow was everywhere. In her hair, in her eyes, on her clothes. She grabbed a handful and smashed it into Cooper's face.

"Yum. A snow cone," he said, grinning down at her. He grabbed a handful and held it over her face, threatening. "Say you'll miss me while I'm gone."

"Oh, that's easy. I'll miss you."

"Promise?"

"Um-hmm. Will you miss me?"

The laughter faded. "Sweetheart, you have no idea how much."

Natalie couldn't resist. She wound her arm around his neck and yanked him down for a kiss to curl his hair and melt the snow away.

Moments later, a bemused Cooper helped her to her feet. "Wow. Keep doing that and I may never make it to Zurich at all."

A cocky quip was forming on her lips when she suddenly realized how quiet the yard had become.

One look at her daughters told her why. Lily was busy rolling a giant ball for another snow person, but Rose was watching Natalie and Cooper. The expression on her face left little doubt about her opinion of the kiss.

"You're both stupid," she yelled and then whirled away, storming toward the house, her red coat a splash against the sea of frozen white.

Cooper's scowl followed Rose's progress across the snowy yard. When he turned that scowl toward Natalie, she felt helpless.

"Aren't you going to do something?"

Natalie shook her head. "I don't know

what to do anymore."

Though he said nothing, his disapproval was obvious.

He was right. Natalie knew he was right, but she felt so helpless. "I'll go talk to her."

Cooper caught her arm. "You've tried that."

Frustration coupled with embarrassment made her say, "Exactly what do you expect me to do? Beat her with a hammer? I can't make her feel something she doesn't."

"But you can make her behave in a respectful manner."

"She isn't a bad kid, Cooper."

"I never said she was." The line of his mouth was hard.

"It sounded like it to me."

"Don't be unreasonable."

"You're the one being unreasonable. Rose is still grieving for Justin."

"And how long are you going to play the martyr to your daughter's grief? Two years? Ten?"

"She's my baby. Helping her through this is my job."

"You aren't helping. You're enabling."

"Enabling?" He made it sound as though Rose was a drug addict instead of a grieving child. "That's the silliest thing I've ever heard."

"Disciplining a child may not be fun or easy, but it is necessary."

"And what would you know about disciplining children?"

"Enough to know no child of mine would ever talk to me the way Rose talks to you and other adults."

"Well, here's a blast for you, Doc." By now Natalie was shaking all over and it had nothing at all to do with the freezing temperature. "She's not your child. You're not her father. So stop trying to be."

Cooper went as still as frozen air. The ugly words pulsed between them. Natalie wanted to snatch them back but it was too late. The damage was done.

"I shouldn't have said that." Natalie reached out, touched his chest. He stepped away.

"Maybe you should have." His voice, hot a moment ago, was now coldly quiet. "Now, at least, I know where I stand."

Before she could find the words to fix what she'd broken, he'd spun on his heel and stalked toward the SUV parked at curbside. Head spinning and heart hurting, Natalie stood as still as the snowman and watched love drive away.

CHAPTER ELEVEN

Cooper forced himself to drive slowly, though his blood raced with adrenaline. Natalie had cut him to the core. She'd driven a knife right through him and left him bleeding in the snow. He should have known. He should have seen it coming.

Though he'd harbored some ill-begotten fantasy about happy ever after, Natalie would never let him past her carefully erected wall of independence. It was *her* life. *Her* children. Justin's family. He was the interloper.

Guts in a knot, he admitted that he'd wanted them to be his children, his family. In spite of her bratty moments, Rose could be funny and appealing and her fierce loyalty to Justin got to him in a big way. And Lily. Well, Lily had won his heart the moment she'd entrusted him with her damaged Barbie.

Natalie's words echoed in his brain, as

haunting as a scream. *You're not her father. You're not her father. You're not her father.*

But he'd wanted to be. He'd wanted not only to take over Justin's responsibility to care for Natalie but to fill Justin's roll as husband and father. And none of it had had anything to do with competition.

He slammed his hand against the leather-covered steering wheel.

He loved her. Didn't she understand that?

A bitter laugh erupted from his throat. All his foolish talk of wanting to take care of her for Justin's sake was a crock. He'd loved Natalie for years, long before she'd come into his life this time. Ten years ago she'd chosen Justin and, rather than face the truth that he loved her, Cooper had escaped to California, pretending Natalie had only been another prize in the long competition between him and Justin. A prize he'd lost.

It had all been a lie concocted to salvage his wounded pride. He saw that now. Part of him had hated his old rival and friend for taking her. No wonder he felt guilty about Justin's death.

Despising himself for the last thought, Cooper aimed the vehicle toward the hospital. There was plenty to do before he flew out tomorrow. He should have kept his mind on the real goals, the attainable. He could be chief in a few years if he'd throw all his energies in that direction. His work was the one constant in his life, the thing that lasted. Whatever had made him think differently?

He pulled into his labeled parking space and exited the SUV, snicking the locks. Head down, he braced against the sharp wind cutting through the garage.

The only sensible thing for him to do was to bow out of Natalie's life for good. He would always be second best to her children's father.

And to a Sullivan, second best was the same as dead last.

Natalie didn't want to cry. What she wanted was to eat the ten pounds of European chocolate she'd ordered for Julie's wedding.

Tears prickled the back of her eyelids. She slashed at them with the heel of her hand. She was not going to cry.

"Mommy." Lily, bottom lip nearly touching the wooden floor, stared up at her with wet gray eyes. "Is Cooper mad at us?"

"Not at you, sweetie. At me."

She was still furious, too. Angry with him and with herself. Why had she believed they could work things out? Why had she let down her guard? For two years she'd stood on her own two feet and done just fine. Well, maybe not fine, but she'd survived.

"He's not going to be our new daddy, is he?"

Natalie nearly went to her knees. Instead, she carefully set a metal mixing bowl onto the counter, controlling every movement. Letting go of her emotions would only upset Lily more. "I don't think so, baby."

How did she explain to a child something she didn't understand herself?

Lily sniffed twice and tears began to roll down her round cheeks. Natalie knelt and took the quivering child into her arms.

"It's okay, sweetie. Mommy's sad, too. But we'll be all right. We were okay before we met Cooper. We'll be okay now."

That was a lie. They weren't okay. They had been going through the motions of life. At least, she had been.

Then Cooper had come along, making her laugh and feel like a woman again. Reminding her of all the things that had been missing in her life. He'd pushed and cajoled and brought his gifts and his smiles until she'd grown dependent on him, not financially but emotionally.

She needed him like cake needed sugar.

Lily's warm breath puffed against her neck. "You were yelling at each other."

241

"I'm sorry. We were upset."

"Because of Rose. She was mean. She says Daddy wouldn't want Cooper to be our new daddy, but that's not true. Daddy loved us. He wanted us to be happy. When Cooper's here, we're like a family again."

Chest heavy, Natalie felt as if she'd swallowed a hot brick. Life had gotten far too complicated for her liking.

"Is Cooper still our friend?" Lily asked.

"I'm sure he is." She wasn't sure of anything.

Lily pulled away. "Can I call him?"

No! Instead she said, "Maybe later." She wiped her daughter's wet cheeks with her fingertips. "Why don't you help me make some fancy frosting for this cake I'm baking. I'll let you pick the colors."

Lily shook her head. "I don't want to."

"I do." Rose bounced into the kitchen as if nothing had transpired.

Natalie couldn't believe the change in her daughter. She actually seemed . . . triumphant.

Was Cooper right? Was she encouraging her child to misbehave?

Natalie shook her head. "I don't think so, Rose. I'm not too happy with you right now."

"Whatever." Rose shrugged and turned

away. "Come on, Lily. Let's play house. I'll let you be the boss."

If she hadn't been so upset, Natalie would have laughed. As it was, she went back to work, baking until the wee hours of the morning. She definitely had some thinking to do.

As she cracked eggs and whisked chocolate, she grumbled and whined and ruminated. She worried and fretted and pondered. Several times she considered calling Regina for advice and commiseration, but the hour was far too late to disturb a pregnant woman.

When she started talking to the invisible dog, she faced the truth. In a real crisis, cake therapy didn't help at all.

The next morning after a restless night filled with confusing dreams, she pulled herself out of bed to get the girls ready for school. Today promised to be a busy day, regardless of her fatigue. She showered and dressed with grim determination.

Cooper was not going to ruin her day. She'd gone on after losing Justin. She'd go on again.

No matter how much it hurt.

To make matters worse, Rose was having one of her mornings. After yesterday Natalie was in no mood to put up with her daughter's negative behavior.

"Get up and get dressed. And don't say one grumpy word."

She might as well have saved her breath. Rose started to cry. "I don't feel good."

Guilt could do that to a person. "I'm not kidding, Rose. I'm tired and cranky myself. Your whining won't work today."

The crying grew worse. "My head hurts. Can I have a drink?"

Exasperated and determined not to give in, Natalie sent Lily for a glass of water while she hunted for the thermometer. "I swear, Rose Isabella, if you don't have a fever, you could be in big trouble."

She didn't have a fever, but by the time Natalie had finished taking her temperature, she wondered if perhaps Rose was telling the truth. Achy and cranky, her eyes were on the glassy side and she complained of a headache.

With Rose she could never be certain, but Natalie wanted to err on the side of caution. After administering children's Tylenol to Rose, she kept both girls home from school. Lily could keep her sister company while Natalie worked.

By ten Rose seemed no better but no worse, either, and Natalie had to run to the shop with samples for a scheduled wedding party. Determining that the lack of fever meant Rose wasn't contagious, she loaded the girls into the van.

Being a single mom was hard. At times like this she missed having a partner so much. A vision of Cooper, strong and dependable, rose up to haunt her.

Just thinking about him brought tears to her eyes.

"You look awful," Julie blurted when she walked into the shop. "Are you sick?"

"Rose is a little under the weather." She tried to divert attention from herself.

Callie swept in from somewhere. "Who's sick?"

"Rose isn't feeling too well," Julie told her. "I think she needs cake and milk."

"Agreed," Callie said. "Preferably chocolate. What did you bring us, Nat?"

Natalie laughed. "Actually, I brought a little of everything. Eight new samples and a brand-new strawberry cheesecake frosting are in the kitchenette."

The other Belles exchanged glances and then turned as a unit to stare at Natalie.

"Is anything wrong?" They all knew of her compulsion to bake when upset. In fact, Belle claimed she was her most creative during a crisis.

"Cooper and I —" She shrugged, not wanting to go into the breakup in front of Rose and Lily, but her eyes filled with unshed tears.

Callie held out a hand to each of the twins. "Come on, girls. Aunt Callie will dish up the goodies while your mom talks to Aunt Belle." She gave Natalie a pointed look. "You will go in and talk to Belle, won't you?"

Her boss appeared in the doorway. "Talk to Belle about what?" She took one look at Natalie and said, "Never mind. Get into my office right this minute before the brides see you and run off screaming."

"That bad, huh?"

"Like a hammered banana."

"Exactly the way I feel," Natalie admitted as she followed Belle into a sun-washed office reminiscent of a Southern sitting room.

"What happened?" Belle sat down next to her in a high backed chair, bringing with her the rich scent of expensive perfume. "Did that handsome boy do something I need to scold him for?"

Natalie shook her head. Even heartsick, she had to smile at Belle's description. Cooper was anything but a boy. In moments she had blurted out the entire story, thankful for the warm, motherly shoulder.

Belle listened without interruption. When Natalie began to cry, Belle took both her hands in hers. "You just go right on and cry, darling child. My mama always said crying washes out the unclear thoughts and lets us see things straight."

"I love him, Belle."

"Well, you can't get much straighter than that." Belle patted her knee. "What are you going to do about it?"

"Nothing I can do. He was the one who walked away."

"Maybe you need to cry some more."

Natalie pulled her hands away and covered her face. "I don't know what you mean."

"Did you ever think that Cooper might be right? That maybe you are a little too easy on Rose?"

"But she's been through so much. I can't bear to see her upset."

"You and Lily have been through the same fire, honey." Cooper had said the same thing. "Loving Rose is healthy, but letting her run the show isn't."

"She's a good girl most of the time."

"She's a precious gem, but even diamonds need a little polish."

"Oh, Belle. I don't know. Things would never work between Cooper and me, anyway. Like Justin he's so obsessed with his career. Plus he has this whole macho idea about taking care of me. I don't need that. I don't want it."

"And why is that so terrible?"

"Justin never let me do anything. He wouldn't let me work. He wouldn't even let me see the monthly bills. After he died, I was stunned to know how much we owed. He thought he was protecting me but in reality, he crippled me."

"We're not talking about Justin."

The simple statement stunned Natalie. She said nothing as Belle went on. "I'm a widow, too, remember? I was married to Matthew for twenty-three years. He was the love of my life and I never expected to find anyone else that even came close. But sometimes love takes you by surprise."

"Charlie?" Natalie asked.

Belle smiled. "We're not talking about me, either. Let's stick to the topic of you and Cooper."

For all her avoidance, Natalie suspected her boss had fallen in love with Charlie Wiley. And she was thrilled to hear it.

"You've got some thinking to do, sugar," Belle said, pushing to her feet. "And I have a meeting with Madeline Westerling, mother of bridezilla, in five minutes." With a soft laugh, Belle enveloped Natalie in one of her warm, perfumed hugs. "You'll make the right decision. I have faith."

Natalie wished she could say the same, although she did feel more positive. Belle had that effect on everyone.

After a stop at the restroom to splash water on her puffy eyes, she headed back to the kitchenette to set up new photos and sampler trays. Lily met her in the hallway. "Rose is sick."

Frowning, Natalie hurried into the small room and found Rose doubled over in pain. "My tummy hurts."

"How much cake did you eat?"

"Two."

"Hu-uh." Lily's blond head shook back and forth. "You ate a bunch."

Natalie's shoulders relaxed a little. If too much cake was the problem, Rose would survive. "Let's go home. You'll feel better soon."

She'd no more than said the words when Rose turned the color of almond paste and bolted toward the bathroom. Natalie followed, holding her child's trembling body while she threw up. When the worst had subsided, she expected Rose to feel better. Instead, her little girl went limp and lethargic in her arms.

"Rose." Natalie washed her face with a

wet paper towel. "Rosie, talk to Mommy."

Breathing heavily, Rose's head lolled to one side. Her eyelids fluttered upward but she seemed unable to focus. A jolt of fear shot through Natalie. This was no ordinary stomach ache.

"Rose. Wake up, baby. What's wrong? Tell me where you hurt. Rose. Rose!"

When her child barely responded, Natalie started to shake. Something was very wrong. If Cooper were here, he'd know. Everything in her wanted to telephone him. He'd come. She knew he would. No matter what their differences, he would come if she needed him. But he had probably already left for Zurich.

"Lily!" she called. Lily, almost as pale as her sister, appeared in the doorway. "Go get Belle or somebody. We need to get Rose to a doctor."

"Cooper's coming."

"What?"

"Don't be mad. I was scared. I called him."

A frisson of relief shuttered through her. She had no time to wonder about his flight to Europe.

"Oh, darling, I'm not mad. I was going to call him myself." No matter what their personal problems, Cooper cared about her children. He wouldn't let her down. "Now, go. Run and tell Belle."

When Lily shot out of the room like a jet, Natalie scooped Rose into her arms and staggered toward the door. It was one of the few times she resented her petite size. She could barely carry her own sick eight-year-old.

"Rose," she murmured, kissing Rose's now flushed face. Limp as noodles, Rose only quivered in response.

Heart jackhammering, knees trembling, Natalie nearly collapsed when Cooper came running toward her.

"What's wrong? What happened?" He took Rose from her and carried her into Belle's office where he laid her on a settee.

Natalie related Rose's symptoms, including the morning's complaints. "After she was sick, she just went limp. And unconscious." Hysteria edged to the surface. "Cooper, my baby is unconscious."

Cooper's hands touched here and there, lifting Rose's eyelid, feeling her pulse, studying her face. Suddenly he leaned forward and tilted her mouth open and sniffed.

"Has she ever been screened for diabetes?"

In that instant Natalie knew what was wrong with her daughter. "Oh, my God. I never saw it coming."

All the times Rose had asked for drinks at night were not ploys to stay up later. The mood swings, tummy aches and claims of not feeling well enough to go to school weren't just a disobedient child. Even the weight loss Natalie had considered a growing spurt were all symptoms a diabetic should have recognized.

"Do you have any insulin with you?"

Hands pressed to her mouth, Natalie could only shake her head as horror rocked her. Rose was a diabetic, and she, a diabetic since childhood, had missed the symptoms. Guilt mixed with abject fear. Her baby could die because of her inattention.

Cooper gathered Rose into his arms. His face was even more grim that it had been yesterday during their fight. "Let's get her to the hospital. Now."

The antiseptic-scented waiting room at Children's was strangely quiet though half a dozen other parents waited with worried expressions. Like hers, their eyes followed every doctor or nurse that passed through, hoping for word.

Belle had offered to come with them, but Natalie had refused, asking instead that she look after Lily. Now she wished she'd allowed one of her friends to come along.

Cooper had disappeared with Rose the moment they'd arrived. She hated waiting alone. It reminded her too much of the day she'd waited for word about Justin.

A flurry of hospital activity flowed around her, doctors in blue scrubs, nurses in cartoon smocks, rattling gurneys and the quiet-voiced paging system. Elevators pinged open, belching out more patients and equipment, yet Natalie felt terribly alone.

When she could bear the strain no longer, she walked to a vending machine. Though she wanted nothing but to know her child would be all right, she stared bleakly at the choices. Remembering that in the rush and panic she'd left her handbag at the shop, she leaned her head against the machine and cried.

A strong hand touched her shoulder. "Hey."

When Cooper turned her gently around, she fell against him. It felt so good to let go, to allow someone else to share the worry.

"Come and sit down before you collapse." He led her gently to a chair, keeping one arm around her shoulders as though fearing she might fly to pieces.

"Is she okay?" Natalie asked through trembling lips.

"The best endocrinologist in Boston is

working with her now." That wasn't the answer she wanted. "Diabetic ketoacidosis is a very dangerous condition."

"I know," she whispered. "Promise me she'll be okay."

He shifted his athletic body so they were facing each other and took both her hands in his. "We do good work here, sweetheart, and Rose is a fighter."

A teary smile pulled at her mouth. "For once it's a good thing."

"Yeah." His face, so full of kindness and compassion, touched her deep inside. She was a fool to let this good, good man walk away.

"I can't believe I didn't recognize the symptoms."

"It happens. Don't beat yourself up about it."

"What if she —" Natalie choked on the fear.

"Don't even go there." His jaw flexed. "Not for one minute."

They sat in silence, waiting. Natalie was certain she would have collapsed into a senseless blob if Cooper hadn't been there. Standing on her own was good. Having a partner at her side was even better.

After what seemed like a lifetime, a tall, narrow man with a shock of white-blond hair came toward them. Cooper made the introductions, then listened, intent and focused, while Dr. Parmeter gave him a rundown of Rose's condition.

Natalie trembled at the frightening tale of chemical imbalance, cardiac arrhythmias, molecular dehydration, and a host of other symptoms that had sent her daughter into shock. She didn't catch it all, but she understood enough.

"One of the main things we have to watch for is cerebral edema," the doctor said. "The next few hours are crucial."

"Swelling of the brain," Cooper murmured though he needn't have. Natalie recognized the term and it scared her out of her mind.

"Once we've passed that crisis, we'll be out of the woods and on the road to full recovery." The doctor patted her shoulder. "She's in good hands."

"Can I see her?"

The doctor glanced at Cooper. "Will you take her back? She looks as if she could use some moral support."

In other words, they thought she'd crash on them. She wouldn't, but Cooper's presence was a strength and comfort she wouldn't refuse. Might as well face it. She needed him like Rose needed insulin. Somehow she had to find a way to tell him that.

Some sort of understanding passed between the two physicians, and the endocrinologist left.

"She's going to look scary, lots of tubes and monitors, so brace yourself."

Natalie bristled. "I do not have hysterics."

"That's my girl." Cooper grinned but she could read his worry. He was shaken, too, by the close call.

With Cooper strong and stalwart by her side, she entered the dim room where machines made swish-swish sounds and monitors ticked and beeped. Rose's eyes were closed and she looked like something from a science fiction movie. Dark eyelashes lay against waxy white cheekbones. Tubes ran from her arms, her nose, her chest, her bladder, and on and on until the horror of the situation was too much for a mother to bear.

Natalie's knees shook so hard she feared falling until Cooper's strong arm circled her waist and drew her tightly against him. After a moment Natalie moved away, bending to kiss her daughter and say all the things she hoped Rose could hear. "I love you. You'll be all right. I love you."

Cooper moved to her side. He said nothing, only lifted Rose's limp, blue-veined hand and kissed it. Natalie felt a splash of love so powerful, tears sprang to her eyes.

When the five minutes were up, she and Cooper returned to the waiting room. All night long Cooper sat beside her, taking the short walk down the hall for visits, bringing her coffee and snacks, telling her stories to occupy her mind while they waited for the crisis to pass and Rose to awaken.

And during that long night of waiting, a new and wonderful truth dawned. She'd been wrong about so many things. About Rose. About herself as a woman who didn't need love or a helpmate. But most of all, she'd been wrong about Cooper. He was strong and dependable and loved her and the girls enough to come running in a crisis even after she'd hurt him.

"Cooper," she murmured, head against his shoulder.

"What, love?"

"Thank you for being here. I needed you so much."

He twisted around to kiss her forehead. "No problem."

"I'm sorry for the things I said."

He was quiet for a moment. "Don't be. You were right. I'm not her father."

"You'd be a good one."

He turned, expression puzzled. She rushed

on, "Even though Rose's diabetes explains some of her erratic behavior, it doesn't take away the fact that I was wrong for the things I said. I want you in my life, Cooper. My girls need you. I need you." She swallowed her last ounce of pride. "Please say you'll forgive me."

He shook his head, slowly, seriously, and Natalie was certain all was lost. "In a crisis like this, a man reevaluates his priorities. I've spent my entire life pursuing the brass ring only to find it loses its luster the moment I have my hands on it. When I received Lily's frantic call, my heart stopped. The world stopped. At first I thought something had happened to you and I knew I would die if that was true. Then seeing Rose lying there unconscious tore me apart. I love being a doctor. I'm good at it. But for the first time, my skills saved someone I love." His mouth twisted in a wry smile. "I love that little girl, Natalie."

"I know you do."

He took her hands and studied the palms as though he could read her lifeline. "Do you also know I love you?"

The thrill of hearing those words was sweeter than any frosting. "I love you, too, Cooper. You're the only man who could make me relinquish my independence again."

His head jerked upward. "Is that what you think I want?"

"Isn't it? Doesn't my little cake business embarrass you?"

A chuckle rumbled in his chest. "We have a lot of talking to do, my love. All I want is you, the way you are. Cakes and weddings and all. Whatever you want to do with your life is fine with me as long as I can be part of it."

Already on emotional overload, Natalie was stunned to silence. Cooper shocked her even more by going to one knee before her.

"I do have a confession to make, though," he said, gently cupping her face. "All my life I have focused on winning. If I wanted something, I never gave up until it was mine. A long time ago, I wanted you. When you came back into my life, you were unfinished business, the prize I'd wanted but never won."

"I suspected that." She started to pull away, but Cooper held fast.

"Hear me out. Please." When she settled again, he went on. "You're the reason I moved to California. I couldn't bear seeing you with another man, though I never told you that. I didn't even know it myself, but you're the reason I'm still single. Natalie, I loved you then and I love you now, not as a prize to win, but as the other half of me that's always been missing."

Tears of exhaustion, of joy, of tenderness sprang to her eyes. "Oh, Cooper."

"You deserve flowers and music and a beautiful setting, and you'll get those, I promise. But right now, this long night would be made much better if you'd put me out of my misery and agree to be my wife."

Natalie braced a hand on either side of Cooper's beloved face. Here was a man who allowed her be herself. He'd accepted her flaws, her desperate need for independence, and her children.

"Oh, yes, I definitely will. I love you, Cooper."

He stood up then and gathered her ever so gently into his arms. "I love you, too, my sweet little cake fairy."

Then his lips touched hers in a kiss far sweeter than any cake she'd ever baked. The wellspring of happiness bubbled up inside until the worry and fatigue of the last hours were momentarily forgotten.

After a moment, she pulled back slightly and said, "I just remembered something. You're supposed to be in Zurich."

He shook his head. "No, love, I'm supposed to be here with you. Zurich will have to wait."

He'd given up this chance to speak at a prestigious conference for her? And that's when she knew without a doubt that Cooper Sullivan loved her even more than his career.

When Natalie was sure her heart would burst through her rib cage and fly away, a nurse breezed into the room and interrupted. "Dr. Sullivan. Ms. Thompson. Rose is awake."

Natalie pulled back, but remained in the protective circle of Cooper's arms. "Oh, thank goodness. Cooper?" She saw her relief reflected in his eyes and loved him all the more. "Can we continue this conversation later?"

He kissed her nose. "Count on it. Now, let's go see our girl."

By midmorning Rose had been moved from ICU to a private room, recovering with expected, but still amazing, rapidity. Cooper was more exhausted than he could remember. He'd been up for more than thirty-six hours. Though he hadn't admitted as much to Natalie, he'd slept none at all after their quarrel and now the vigil with Rose had about done him in.

But through the haze of fatigue, a new song played in his heart. Natalie loved him. The most awesome realization was that he loved her, completely, fully, without strings. He felt free, though he'd never understood before that he was a captive of his own ambition. Natalie's love had changed him from a shell of a man grasping at success. Now he knew what success really meant. It wasn't being chief of surgery. It wasn't being the next senator or the top student. Success was in loving. Plain and simple.

"Cooper." Next to Rose's bed, Natalie sat on the chair between his thighs, her back to him, his arms around her waist. He relished the feel of her small body rested against his, the sweet scent of her skin in his nostrils. Some primal, protective urge had surfaced yesterday and he experienced an unquenchable need to touch her, to keep her safe.

"What, love?" he murmured, nuzzling the back of her hair.

"You need to go home and get some rest."

"I'm fine."

"You were snoring."

"I was not."

She laughed, a tired, but happy sound. "I love you."

"Feeling's mutual. Turn around here and kiss me."

With a tired chuckle, she slid her slender arms around his neck and rocked his world.

He was drowning in pure joy and manly needs, his mind quickly going to places it shouldn't, when the sound of giggles penetrated his consciousness.

"You two look cozy."

Bearing balloons and teddy bears, a gaggle of wedding planners stood in the doorway. Natalie slid off Cooper's lap, blushing.

"Oh, you guys." Fed by exhaustion and stress, emotion gushed from Natalie. "Thank you so much for coming."

"We brought a worried little girl to see you and Rose." Lily had spent the night with Regina. Eyes wide and serious, she rushed into her mother's arms.

"She's okay, baby. Go on over and see her. She's still sleeping a lot but she'll wake up for you."

Lily went to the bed and stood staring down at her sister. "Rose."

Rose opened her eyes. "I have to take shots now, like Mom."

Lily's gaze flickered to her mother. "That's right, honey. But don't worry. Taking shots is a piece of cake."

The gathered group chuckled at the joke.

"Cooper saved my life," she told Lily. "That's what the nurse said."

Lily leaned close to whisper. "Do you still hate him?"

Rose shook her head from side to side, her voice soft. "Not anymore. Daddy came last night. He gave me some medicine, then he had to go. But he said not to be sad anymore, because Cooper was here now and he would take good care of us and Mommy."

The adults exchanged startled looks. Natalie mouthed, "A dream?"

With a puzzled shrug, Cooper drew his lady beneath the shelter of his arm. In his career, he'd witnessed stranger things. But, be it a dream or something real, Rose believed Justin had given his blessing. Maybe he had. A good man had left behind three treasures, and now they were Cooper's to love and protect.

With a grateful heart and everything in him, Cooper vowed never to let his old friend down.

EPILOGUE

A cold wind blew in off the ocean, but even inclement weather could not dampen Natalie's happiness. She and the girls were riding with Cooper to some mysterious destination, and the excitement wafting off him in waves was enough to fuel her curiosity and her own excitement.

The last week and a half had been nothing short of wonderful. Rose had recovered and was learning to check her own blood sugar in the same way Natalie did. While she regretted passing the malady on to her child, Natalie was glad to see Rose returning to the happy little girl she'd once been.

Part of that had been Cooper's doing. He'd gone out of his way to woo the twins, with both love and fatherly guidance.

She reached across the seat and placed a hand on his thigh. He glanced her way and then grinned down at her hand. "Better be careful. You'll start a fire you can't put out."

"Oh, I can put it out."

He laughed. "But you won't."

"Soon." They'd been debating the when, where and how of getting married since Rose's dismissal from the hospital. Both of them wanted to marry sooner rather than later, but with her wedding commitments and his work, finding time was an issue. "When are you going to tell us where we're going?"

With a flick of his wrist, he turned the steering wheel and headed down a side street. "Right about . . . now."

He pulled into a lovely circular driveway in front of a stunning three-story Victorian home and shut off the engine. He turned in his seat, smiling. "What do you think?"

"It's glorious."

"Let's go inside. You're going to love it. Everything's been modernized and renovated while keeping the integrity of the architecture."

"You sound like a real estate agent."

He laughed and got out. The twins were already barreling onto the long porch.

Once inside, she understood his enthusiasm even better. The home was spectacular, the kind of place she'd always dreamed of.

When they stopped in the kitchen, an eerie feeling drifted over her. The enormous room had been outfitted with all the modern amenities that any baker could covet, including two giant ovens and bakers' racks. She ran her fingertips over the stainless steel finish. "Cooper, what have you done? What is this?"

"You said you wanted a big house with a backyard and plenty of room for the girls to play. So —" he thrust his arms out to either side "— I bought us one."

He'd remembered that? Her mouth fell open, making him laugh.

"You like?"

"I love. And I love you." She flung herself into his arms.

He rocked her back and forth, chest rumbling with happiness. "I was so worried you wouldn't like it or you'd think I was trying to control your life or steal your independence."

"I'm past that now, Cooper."

"If you hate it, we'll sell it."

"Don't you dare! I love this place. It's perfect."

"Good. I was hoping you'd say that. The sooner I find you a house, the sooner I can get you married and into my bed."

She whacked his shoulder, then gave it up and kissed him again, holding back nothing. Being in Cooper's arms was the best place she'd ever been.

"Are we buying this house?" Lily asked as she thumped down the stairs and headed for the back door.

"We already did."

"Yes!" She disappeared through a sun-washed living area to relay the news just as Rose ran breathlessly into the kitchen.

"Mom, Mom, you gotta come out here. Come on. Come see."

She grabbed a hand of each adult and pulled toward the wide back doors where Lily waited on the porch, an Irish setter sitting beside her, adoration in his golden eyes.

"We found this dog out here. Isn't she beautiful?"

"His name is Chauncey," Cooper said. "He belongs to a friend of mine who is moving away and can't keep him. Right now, he's looking for a new owner."

Rose's face lit up. "We'll take him."

"Oh, I don't know. That's a big responsibility. Who will feed him?"

The picture of hope, Rose threw her arms around the dog's neck and buried her face in the gleaming red coat. "I will. I've had experience."

Natalie choked back the laugh. The invisible biting dog was not experience.

Rose leaned in to kiss the dog and received

a lick on the cheek. "See, he likes me. Please, please, please, can I keep him?"

"A big yard like this needs a good dog," Lily put in from her spot on the opposite side of the tail-thumping setter.

Natalie looked at Cooper and knew what he was up to. "Trying to replace the lovely and endearing invisible Puppy?"

"What do you think?"

"I think you just sealed your fate." She looped an arm around his waist.

"Meaning?"

"Meaning you have to marry us now for certain. The house, the dog, the kitchen. I gotta have them all."

"What about the guy?"

"Mmm, let me think." She touched her chin in mock consideration. "Oh, yeah. I think I'll take him, too."

He heaved a sigh so loud, the twins looked up.

"In that case," he said, reaching into his inner jacket. "Here you go. My wedding present to you. A little early maybe, but it's done."

Natalie took the envelope and removed a sheaf of papers. The deed to the property was on top. Beneath it was Cooper's life insurance policy. Both were in her name.

Tears pricked her eyes. "You didn't have

to do this."

He gathered her close. "No matter what life brings, you and the girls are taken care of. Not that I'm planning on going anywhere for a long time, but I want you to feel secure."

"I don't know what to say. It's too much. I have nothing to give you in return."

"That's where you're wrong, my love." He tenderly stroked her hair. "All these years I've searched for something. I didn't know until now but that something was you. Not success, not being the best of the best. You, with your sweet love. I was empty. Now I'm filled. And that's worth more than all the things we'll ever buy."

A feeling of serene peace settled over Natalie as she rested her head against Cooper's strong, steady heartbeat. Cooper, too, had given her far more than financial security. He'd given her the freedom to be a woman again.

Out in the fenced backyard, her children — soon to be his, as well — played happily with the dog of their dreams. Here in Cooper's arms, all her own dreams were coming true. Dreams she hadn't even dared to dream.

She'd never expected to be happy again, to love again, to feel safe again. What a fortunate woman she was to have been loved by one good man and now another. Somehow she knew Justin would approve.

The wind swirled through the backyard and tussled her daughters' hair. One of them laughed and the pure, childish joy said it all.

Here in this big house with this loving man, she and the twins would make a new start, a new life. Yes, she was a blessed woman.

She reached up and touched Cooper's face, saw the love in his brilliant eyes and knew a truth so deep and wonderful, she had to laugh with joy.

Her life was sweeter than a five-layer cake and Cooper Sullivan was the icing on top.

We hope you have enjoyed this Large Print book. Other Thorndike, Wheeler, and Chivers Press Large Print books are available at your library or directly from the publishers.

For information about current and upcoming titles, please call or write, without obligation, to:

Publisher
Thorndike Press
295 Kennedy Memorial Drive
Waterville, ME 04901
Tel. (800) 223-1244

or visit our Web site at:

http://gale.cengage.com/thorndike

OR

Chivers Large Print
published by BBC Audiobooks Ltd
St James House, The Square
Lower Bristol Road
Bath BA2 3SB
England
Tel. +44(0) 800 136919
email: bbcaudiobooks@bbc.co.uk
www.bbcaudiobooks.co.uk

All our Large Print titles are designed for easy reading, and all our books are made to last.